FRIEND OR FOE?

Isabel took a step toward the door, then Adam grabbed her arm.

"I don't have time for this," she muttered. She tried to pull her arm away, but Adam tightened his grip, digging his fingers into her bare skin.

And then they were connected. But it wasn't like any connection she'd ever experienced. This was a violation. The images were being ripped from her mind.

She tried to scream, but the muscles in her throat contracted, as if they'd been squeezed by a hand jammed down her mouth.

A flood of images pounded into Isabel. Too many. Too much. Blasting her raw brain.

She opened her lips again. "Michael." She forced the word through her bruised throat. "Michael, help. Please . . ."

Don't miss any books in this fascinating new series:

ROSWELL
HIGH

#1 THE OUTSIDER
#2 THE WILD ONE
#3 THE SEEKER
#4 THE WATCHER
#5 THE INTRUDER
#6 THE STOWAWAY
#7 THE VANISHED*
#8 THE REBEL*
#9 THE DARK ONE*
#10 THE SALVATION*

Available from POCKET PULSE
*Coming soon

ROSWELL
HIGH

THE STOWAWAY

by

MELINDA METZ

POCKET
PULSE

POCKET PULSE

New York   London   Toronto   Sydney   Singapore

This book is a work of fiction. Although the physical setting of the book is Roswell, New Mexico, the high school and its students, names, characters, places, and incidents are products of the author's imagination or are used fictitiously. Any resemblance to actual events or locales or persons living or dead is entirely coincidental.

An *Original* Publication of POCKET BOOKS

POCKET PULSE published by
Pocket Books, a division of Simon & Schuster Inc.
1230 Avenue of the Americas, New York, NY 10020

Produced by 17th Street Productions, Inc.
33 West 17th Street
New York, NY 10011

ISBN: 0-671-02379-9

First Pocket Pulse printing April 2000

10 9 8 7 6 5 4 3 2 1

POCKET PULSE and colophon are trademarks of
Simon & Schuster Inc.

Printed in the U.S.A.

"He almost killed us! I can't believe you're defending him," Max Evans yelled, his bright blue eyes burning as he glared at Michael Guerin.

Michael leaned his head against the cave's cool limestone wall, trying to get a grip on the anger building inside him. Now wasn't the time to go off. Max was his best friend. There had to be a way to get him to listen, to understand. "Agreed, Adam almost killed us," Michael answered, fighting to keep his voice low and calm. "All I'm saying is that—"

"There's nothing else *to* say," Max interrupted.

"And of course *you're* the one who gets to decide that, right?" Michael asked. "What about Liz and Maria and Isabel? Or Cameron? Can't they speak here?"

Cameron Winger, who had been sitting quietly against the wall, looked up at the others and spoke. "I don't want to be involved in your Psychic Friends Network discussion. It just doesn't involve me," she said.

No one said anything. Max looked furious.

Michael glanced around the circle. His eyes

1

locked on Max's sister, Isabel. More than any of the others, she should have a little sympathy for Adam. Adam had lived out her worst nightmare—he'd spent almost his entire life locked away in Project Clean Slate's underground compound, never even allowed to see the sun. Just because he happened to come from another planet. Just because he was one of them.

"It could have been you who grew up in the compound, Izzy," he reminded her. The color drained from Isabel's face, even her lips getting all pinched and white. Michael knew he was hurting her, but he forced himself to go on. "You, and Max, and me, we just got lucky. Our incubation pods were moved to the cave before the Project Clean Slate guys showed up at the crash site. We've always had each other. Adam grew up without anyone around who was . . . like him." Michael's words tumbled out faster and faster. "He's one of us. We've got to help him. There's got to be something wrong with him. He's sick or something. I know Adam. He would never have tried to hurt anyone—"

"Michael, you knew him for what, three days when you were in the compound together?" Liz Ortecho asked, cutting him off. "I knew him about that long, too. And I liked him. I did. But who knows what the Project Clean Slate people did to him? Maybe they were able to turn him into some kind of living weapon or something."

"That makes no sense," Michael shot back. He could hear the anger in his voice, and he clamped down on it hard. The situation here could turn ugly . . . fast. He could feel it. And he wasn't going to let the group shatter because they couldn't come to an agreement about what to do with Adam. But he also wasn't going to allow anyone to create some new kind of prison for Adam, either.

That meant he had to be careful, to think before he spoke. Remember, Liz is a science head, just like Max, he told himself. If you want her on your side, you have to give her a logical argument. "Look, if Sheriff Valenti and his Clean Slate gang had brain-washed Adam to make him an alien assassin, they wouldn't have included 'kill Sheriff Valenti!' in the mental program. It wouldn't make any sense."

"Okay, you're right," she agreed. "But here's the thing." She twisted her long dark hair into a knot on top of her head, then immediately let it fall free. "For some reason, Adam tried to kill Max tonight. He *did* kill Valenti. And he torched the compound, which is pretty much the same as trying to kill all of us. Bottom line is, he's dangerous. And with his powers, we can't defend ourselves against him. Well, maybe you and Max and Isabel can. But he seems to have powers that are much more developed than yours."

"I've seen this episode before," Cameron announced suddenly. She shoved herself to her feet and wandered toward the back of the cave.

Michael wasn't exactly surprised. He'd only known Cameron for about a week, but she'd immediately made it clear she had zero tolerance for bull. In fact, there was something sexy about her sassiness.

"Why is she even here, anyway?" Isabel complained, not bothering to lower her voice. "Doesn't she have a home?"

Michael knew the answer to that one. Yeah, Cameron had a home in some other state. A home she never wanted to go back to. A home that was so bad, she'd agreed to submit to tests at the compound as long as Valenti promised not to tell her parents where she was.

But that was Cameron's story to tell. Or not.

"Adam said she was in a cell near yours," Maria DeLuca whispered. "Does that mean she's a . . ." She shot a glance at Michael. It was the first time she'd managed to look at him since she and the others had broken into the compound to rescue him. Michael knew she must feel strange—there was definitely some unfinished business between them. Business Michael wasn't looking forward to finishing. Maria had told him she loved him right before he got captured. Since he'd basically been in prison, he'd gotten away with not saying much of anything in response to the L word. But now he was out, and sooner or later . . .

Later, Michael thought. Much later. Even for the most sensitive of guys, which he never claimed

4

to be, now was not the time to deal with Maria and her feelings.

"Valenti was having one of the doctors do some experiments on Cameron," he answered. "She has some parapsychological powers. I don't know how or why or even what exactly. But I know for sure that she's not one of *us.*"

"You mean, one of you alien freaks?" Maria asked, her head tilted like a curious dog.

Max snorted, then broke into a chuckle. Maria and Isabel started giggling. Yeah, Michael thought. This feels more like *normal.*

"Look, why don't we go around the circle and each say what we think we should do about Adam," Liz suggested. "No yelling. No interrupting each other. Everyone gets a turn. Then we make a decision."

"I'll go first. I think we should sedate Adam until we know for sure what his deal is," Max said. "Maybe I can get some info from the collective consciousness to find out a way to do it without hurting him."

The collective consciousness. Michael hadn't even had a chance to ask Max what it was like. Max had made the connection while Michael was in the compound. Michael knew that it was like tapping your mind into the mind and experiences of an entire planetful of people and that it would increase Max's powers tenfold. But how? Man, it felt like he'd been trapped in the compound half his life, even though it had really only been about a week.

Everyone seemed a little different somehow. Especially Max. He couldn't believe Max was talking about "sedating" Adam. He sounded like some kind of mad professor.

"You want to keep him blacked out? You? The guy who practically cries when he sees a sick mouse?" Michael snapped.

"I'm thinking about the safety of—," Max began.

"Enough!" Liz cried. "We said no interruptions. Max told us what he thought. I agree with him. I think we'd all be in danger if there was even the possibility Adam could turn his powers on us. Now, Michael, you go."

"I think one of us should be with Adam all the time," he answered. "And that's it. No prison. And no lobotomy."

"I never said anything about—," Max interrupted again.

"Maria, you're up," Liz said.

"Adam lived his whole life in prison," Maria answered. "I don't want to put him in another one. I think we should talk to him. Maybe he has an explanation for what he did. We haven't even asked him."

"We couldn't have," Liz reminded her. "He practically passed out as soon as he got out of the compound."

"After he burned it down, you mean," Max muttered.

"Wait a minute. We're breaking the rules again," Liz said. "Maria, are you done?"

"I just think he deserves the chance to tell his side before we do anything," she said. "No prison. No sedation."

"Okay, Isabel, you go," Liz instructed.

"I agree with Michael," she replied. "I think Adam just went a little nuts when he got back into the compound. Sheriff Valenti made Adam call him Dad. He acted like he loved Adam. Then Adam finds out Valenti didn't love him, that he was using him for his stupid little tests. I would have wanted to kill him, too. And burn down the place that used to be my prison. If I'd been kept there my whole life, I would do whatever it took to make sure no one ever put me back there again."

Isabel pulled in a deep, shuddering breath. "But it's over," she continued. "Adam knows he's safe now. We have no reason to think he'd do anything like that again."

"Except the rabbit," Max said. "He wasn't in the compound when he tried to kill it."

"It was a rabbit, okay?" Isabel shot back. "Yeah, they're cute with their fluffy fur and their big ears and their cotton ball tails. But face it, they're basically rodents."

"Forget the rabbit. What about Max? Are you saying Adam went so crazy in the compound, he didn't know he was trying to kill one of his

7

friends?" Liz exclaimed, her voice tight with emotion.

"You said it was right after he incinerated Valenti," Isabel said. "Maybe Adam just lost control of his power for a second."

"No way. You weren't there. You didn't see him. He wanted to kill me, and he knew exactly who I was. He also knew torching the compound meant we'd all burn with it, and he was happy about it. He wasn't having some kind of post-traumatic stress reaction, if that's what you're thinking," Max insisted.

"And how, exactly, does one look with post-traumatic stress?" Isabel challenged her big brother.

"All right. All right. We've all had our turn," Michael jumped in before Max and Isabel could really start going at each other. "The majority says Adam doesn't need to be restrained at all. He just needs to be with one of us all the time."

"Alex didn't get to vote," Max reminded him. Alex Manes was over at the UFO museum, watching Adam. "I'm still concerned about the fact that we left him alone with Adam."

"Adam's practically in a coma," Michael reminded him. "Alex is perfectly safe."

"There's something else," Liz added softly. "I don't know if I should even say it, but I'm going to." She gave Maria a long, steady look, then turned her gaze to Isabel. "I think you two are being influenced by your feelings for Michael."

You *two*. That meant . . . Michael snapped his head

toward Isabel. Did she have feelings for him, too?

"Oh, right. Love means never having a thought of your own," Isabel snapped. "I'm so sure that's why you agreed with Max, right?"

"I agreed with Max because I—"

Michael tuned out the rest of what Liz was saying. He couldn't believe this. Isabel *and* Maria? What was going on? Isabel was like a sister to him. He glanced back at Cameron to see if she was smiling sarcastically, but she was nowhere in sight. He forced his attention back to Liz.

"All I'm saying is I'd like to hear your answers again after Michael makes some kind of choice between the two of you," she finished.

Michael shoved his hands through his spiky black hair and lowered his gaze to the cave floor. What was *he* supposed to do? Did Liz really expect him to choose? I'll have one Isabel, a Maria, and *two* Camerons to go, he thought. Speaking of Cameron . . .

Michael noticed a green-purple light glistening on the floor, and it was exuding a burning, evil aura. He'd seen that color only one time before. He sprang to his feet.

"What's wrong, Michael?" Isabel asked.

He sprinted to the back of the cave and turned right. There was Cameron sitting on the ground . . . staring wide-eyed at her glowing hands. In her hands lay the ring with the Stone of Midnight. Her face and the wall behind were an eerie shade of green.

A horrifying image filled Michael's mind. Maria lying unconscious on the floor—pale, cold, and dying— with that evil ring on a string around her neck. He wasn't going to let that happen to Cameron.

He hurled himself across the cave at her. Cameron jerked away in surprise, but Michael caught her arm and yanked, sending the ring flying across the stone floor. She flashed him a pained expression, as if her favorite toy had been taken.

"Don't ever touch that again," he ordered. He snatched up the ring and returned it to the metal box they kept it in. Next time he came out here, he was slapping a lock on the thing.

He straightened up and turned back to face Cameron. She raised her eyebrows in an I'm-waiting kind of way.

"The stone in that ring was stolen from our planet," he told her. "When you use its power, it sends out a signal to a group of . . . bounty hunters. Also aliens, but not like us. Let's just say that they aren't guys you'd want to party with."

"How do you know?" Cameron answered. "My taste might be on the kinky side, and I . . ." Her words trailed off.

Michael realized that tiny tremors were running through her body. He reached out and pulled her to him. She held herself stiff, her arms straight at her sides. He figured she was busy cursing herself for looking like a wimp. She prided herself on being tough.

Michael knew a little bit about that, so he didn't bother telling her that he'd do anything he had to for her to be safe. He didn't bother telling her anything. He just held her tight.

And a few moments later he felt her hands dig into the back of his jacket. Slowly the tremors stopped. And Cameron shoved him away. "The floor show's over," she called to the others without looking at them. She headed over to the sleeping bag Michael kept in the corner for the nights he couldn't deal with life as a foster kid. He thought about following but decided that would truly annoy her. Besides, they still hadn't agreed on what to do about Adam.

He turned back to his friends and found himself pinned by two pairs of blue eyes—Maria's hurt, Isabel's challenging.

Oh, great. He cleared his throat. "So, what were we saying?" he asked.

"We were saying that you have no problem with the possibility that Adam might go off again and turn us all into a big pile of ashes," Max answered.

"How's this?" Michael suggested. "No sedation. Adam stays in the museum. Doesn't go out in public. One of us is always with him."

Max frowned. "I don't like it. At all. But it doesn't

seem like I have much of a choice." He rubbed his face with his fingers. "The guards should be our resident aliens—you, me, and Isabel. Two of us should be on him all the time. That way if anything . . . happens, we can combine our power and at least have a chance of dealing with Adam."

Michael nodded. He was afraid if he opened his mouth, Max was really not going to like what he heard. At all.

"I could go with that," Liz said, sounding reluctant.

"Me too," Isabel agreed.

"Yeah," Maria answered. "And while he's there, we talk to him about what happened."

Michael shot a glance over his shoulder at Cameron. She was stretched out on her side, facing away from them. "How would you feel about Cameron staying there, too?" he asked softly. "She doesn't have anyplace else to go."

"As long as there are always two of us on Adam, fine," Max answered.

No one else said anything, which Michael decided to take as a unanimous yes.

"Let's head back," Liz said. "I don't want Alex to be alone with Adam when he comes to."

"Good idea." Michael jumped on the big rock to climb out of the cave.

Max stepped over to him. "There's one more thing I want to say to you," he began, his voice low enough that only Michael could hear it.

Michael knew what was coming next. One of Max's I-love-you-man moments. "We're not going to have to hug or anything, are we?" Michael joked. "I mean, I'm glad you're still alive. You're glad I'm still alive. But we're guys. We—"

"What I wanted to say is that I think you're wrong about Adam," Max interrupted. "And if he does anything to hurt anyone, I'm holding you responsible."

Alex glanced at his watch, then immediately returned his gaze to Adam. Not that the guy had moved for the past hour. When they got to the museum, Alex had practically had to carry Adam inside. He'd dumped him on the couch by the information counter, and Adam hadn't even twitched a finger since then.

Alex definitely wasn't complaining. It's not like he'd been hoping they could shoot some hoops or anything. Basically, he'd been hoping that Adam wouldn't toast him the way he'd toasted Valenti. And it looked like this was his lucky day. Yeah, Alex was going to get through this stretch of guard duty with his pale, freckled hide unsinged. The others should be back soon, and Adam would probably still be zonked.

The others. That meant Isabel. Well, he could cut out once they showed up. He wouldn't have to endure too many minutes of Isabel contact. It hadn't been so bad when the two of them were in the middle of breaking Michael out of the compound. When the walls were bursting into flames around you, you didn't have time to think, Hey, this girl running for her life next to me is the one who just stomped on my heart.

But now that they had all survived, Isabel really wasn't someone he wanted to spend any quality time with.

Not that Isabel wanted to spend any time with him, either. That was pretty much the reason she broke up with him, right? A girl didn't break up with a guy because she really wished they could spend more—

Oh, just shut up, you whiner, Alex ordered himself. She did you a favor. The girl's an ice sculpture, cold to the core.

And beautiful. And willing to do anything to save the lives of the people she loved. And—

A small squeaking sound jolted Alex out of his thoughts. The saliva evaporated from his mouth as he realized the sound was coming from the old leather of the couch. Adam was waking up.

Before Alex could make a move or even decide what move he *should* make, Adam rose from the sofa in one fluid motion. Why didn't I find the fire extinguisher when I had the chance? Alex thought wildly.

"So, Adam, uh, how're you doing?" he asked. "I thought we could go upstairs and watch TV. Maybe make some toast. I know you like toast, right?"

Oh, perfect. Of all things, I had to mention toast, Alex thought.

But Adam didn't answer. He didn't react at all. He stared straight ahead, his green eyes as lifeless as a couple of painted Ping-Pong balls. Lights on, but nobody home.

Alex had no clue what Adam would do next. Which meant it might be a very good idea just to knock him out right now. Alex took a quick glance around. There was a three-foot-high ceramic alien almost within reach. He could grab it, swing it up and around, and connect with Adam's head.

But if he did that, he better make sure to make it an out-of-the-ballpark swing because if Adam didn't lose consciousness instantly, he'd be able to heal himself in about two seconds. And then Alex would be doing his impression of the world's biggest piece of burnt toast.

Pass.

"Or if you're not in the mood for TV, we could do something else," Alex burst out. "Like, uh, we could stand here and see how much sweat my body is able to produce." He tried to laugh, but all he could squeeze out was a weird barking sound.

Adam didn't seem to notice—he was still in zombie mode.

Without a word, Adam turned on his heel and strode behind the information counter. He slid out one of the drawers and dumped the contents on the counter in front of him. His eyes flicked over the paper clips, scissors, tape, staples, pens, and rubber bands, then he swept everything onto the floor. Immediately he yanked out another drawer. Dumped it. Scanned. And swept the countertop clean again. Third drawer. Same deal.

Bizarre.

Adam knelt down and flicked open the double doors of the big cabinet under the drawers. Alex took two steps closer and watched Adam yank out a half-empty box of museum maps, a couple of rhinestone-studded jumpsuits, a first-aid kit, and a bucket of cleaning stuff.

A low growl of frustration escaped Adam's throat. He thrust himself to his feet. Without hesitation he turned to the double row of bookshelves behind him. In an instant the complete collection of UFO books was on the floor.

This was bizarre. Alex was too intrigued to say anything. If Adam wanted to indulge in a little rock-star-in-a-hotel-room action, cool. Alex was up for anything that would keep Adam occupied until some kind of backup arrived.

From the bookshelves he worked his way down the closest wall, tearing each framed photograph off the wall and ripping open the back. That brought him to the little coffee shop. Adam felt under each of the tables and chairs and tossed the contents of the cabinets in the kitchen.

Alex just watched. He felt like an idiot. No, more like a wuss. Ray Iburg had loved this place, and Alex wasn't doing a thing to stop Adam from destroying it.

But Ray was dead, and Alex was hoping to live long enough to at least graduate. So he trailed after Adam like a pathetic little puppy, not saying a word as Adam worked his way to the front of the museum, darting from photo to photo, pulling the back out of each one. When the last one was on the floor, glass shattered, Adam bolted for the spiral staircase leading up to Ray Iburg's apartment.

Alex followed. He watched as Adam yanked the drawers out of Ray's dresser and dumped them. He watched as Adam shoved the mattress off Ray's bed and ran his fingers over every inch. He watched as Adam did an anticleaning job on Ray's closet.

It didn't take Sherlock Holmes to realize he was searching for something—apparently something little. And something very important to Adam. Important enough to squeeze every toothpaste tube in Ray's bathroom. Important enough to empty every box of cereal in Ray's kitchen. Important enough to slit open every beanbag chair in Ray's living room.

Alex's stomach clenched as Adam hurled the last empty plastic beanbag skin to the floor. This was it. Adam had searched every inch of the place. Now what was he going to do?

He turned toward Alex and spoke for the first time since he'd gotten up from the couch. "I need to know where Ray Iburg would have kept anything valuable," he demanded.

Alex decided this was not the time to show any kind of intimidation. He stepped up to Adam and forced himself to look right into his empty eyes. "You've trashed his museum. You've trashed his apartment. Whatever it is you're looking for, it's not here, all right? It's not here!"

Adam blinked once. Then he collapsed into a heap on the floor, like a puppet whose strings had been cut.

Maria leaned against the closest locker and opened her algebra book. No, that didn't look casual and cool. It looked dorky. She sighed and stuffed the book into her backpack.

Just give it up, she told herself. It's not like Michael's ever going to believe you just somehow happened to be hanging out two feet away from his homeroom door one minute before the bell rings. He's going to know you're waiting for him.

At least I'll get to him before Isabel, Maria thought. Duh! Spoke too soon. Seeing Isabel coming her way down the hallway, Maria dropped down on one knee. She untied the lace of her boot and retied it in a double knot, keeping her head as close to her toes as she could get it. Just let her walk on by, she silently begged.

She didn't know who she was begging to, exactly. Not God. She knew she really shouldn't be asking God for stuff like that. People were starving. People were dying. God really didn't have the time for things like making sure Maria was spared a little humiliation.

Please just let her walk on by, Maria begged again. If she had to look at Isabel, she didn't know if she'd be able to go through with the plan she'd come up with last night. The plan where she found Michael before school and told him that Liz was right, that he really did need to choose between her and Isabel—and fast because that was the only way Maria would be able to hang on to the single strand of sanity she had left.

No, if she had to look at Isabel, Isabel with her perfect body, and her perfect hair, and her perfect skin, Maria would lose her nerve. How could she even think about asking Michael to choose between her and all that perfectness?

Maria jerked on the knot she'd just made. She wanted to untie and retie it one more time to make completely sure Isabel had passed her before she stood up. The knot wouldn't come loose. She picked at it, and the nail on her ring finger broke.

Oh, great. Now she'd have to ask Michael to choose between her and Princess Isabel while one of Maria's fingers looked like—

"Hi, Maria."

Even Isabel's voice was perfect, low and a little throaty. Sexy. Guys would definitely think it was sexy.

Maria pushed herself to her feet. "Hey," she mumbled. She couldn't stop herself from checking out Isabel's hands. Every French-manicured nail was perfect, of course. If Isabel ever broke a nail, she could just use her powers to heal it.

You're totally delusional if you think guys ever look at her fingernails, anyway, Maria told herself. Maybe they occasionally look at your nails, but that's only because you don't have quite as many interesting body parts to look at as Isabel does. Well, you *have* them, sort of, but they aren't—

"He's at the museum," Isabel said.

"Who?" Maria asked. Isabel raised one eyebrow in response, and Maria felt heat flood from her hairline all the way down her neck. "Oh, well, I just wanted to tell him welcome back. I didn't really get to talk to him yesterday," she explained, tripping over her words.

"I'll tell him for you," Isabel answered. "I have guard duty with him tonight. All night." She gave Maria a little wave and continued down the hall. More than one guy's head turned as she passed.

Maria turned and rushed down the hall in the opposite direction. When she reached the main doors, she burst through and bolted across the quad. She didn't stop running until she got to the bus stop. She was going to the museum. Now. She had to. She had to talk to Michael before Isabel had guard duty with him. All night.

She yanked open her crocheted purse and dug around for a vial of her cedar oil. She needed to calm down. She didn't want to go flying into the museum and start babbling like an escaped lunatic. Her fingers closed on one of the little vials of aromatherapy oil. She pulled it out. Yes, it was cedar.

It was also empty. That figured. The last few weeks hadn't been exactly stress-free—with Ray Iburg getting killed by Sheriff Valenti, Max almost dying, and Michael getting captured, not to mention Maria telling Michael she loved him and Michael saying basically *nothing* in return. Maria pulled the cap off the vial and took a couple of deep breaths, hoping to get some fumes at least.

When the bus pulled up, she quickly jammed the vial back into her bag. Adults usually did not have good reactions to seeing teenagers with little vials near their noses. As if Maria would ever put anything close to a drug in her body.

The bus's doors opened with a whooshing sound. Maria climbed on and found a seat. She leaned her head against the window and stared out at the long row of fast-food joints and strip malls lining the north end of Roswell's main street. It would take about ten minutes to get to the museum, with all the bus's stops and starts. She decided to use the time to figure out exactly how to say what she wanted to say.

Michael, I can't have any kind of normal life until you decide between me and Isabel—

Too needy.

Michael, be a man. Choose. Now. Or lose me forever.

Yeah, right.

Michael, our friendship is really important to me. And so is my friendship with Isabel. And I know your friendship with Isabel is also very important. I think we're in a situation where all those very important friendships are in danger of—

Too guidance counselor.

Maria banged her head against the window a couple of times. She didn't have much more time to think of something. This was what she should have been doing last night instead of writing that essay on *Julius Caesar.*

Michael, Michael, Michael, lend me your ears. I come to bury Isabel, not to praise her.

Way too retarded.

Only one more stop. Okay, she thought. Okay, okay. I will come up with the exact right thing this time.

Michael, Isabel took me into one of your dreams. I saw you hugging her. The dream made it pretty clear that you're . . . that you have feelings for her. And that's totally cool. I just need you to tell me if—

The bus pulled to a stop in front of the museum. Maria sucked in a deep breath and climbed off. She'd just have to wing it. She hurried to the museum's back entrance, not wanting to lose her nerve. The door was open, so she slipped inside. Pieces of broken glass crunched under her feet as she made her way to the spiral staircase leading to Ray's apartment.

Michael, I . . . , she thought as she started up. Michael, I—Michael, I— It was like her brain had a stutter. That's all she could think. Just Michael, I—

Maria took another step, her head now high enough to see the living-room floor. Her eyes locked onto two pairs of feet. Feet standing very close together.

She tilted back her head and saw that the feet belonged to Michael and that Cameron girl. Their bodies were close together, too. And Michael was giving her that killer smile of his. The one that turned Maria's insides to warm goo.

What was he doing? He should be sitting off in a corner making a list of all the things he liked about Maria and all the things he liked about Isabel, doing the whole compare-and-contrast thing.

Instead he was standing there flirting with a girl he'd known for, what, a week? Maria hadn't liked the way Michael hugged Cameron yesterday, but she figured it was no big deal. Cameron was freaked. Michael was a nice guy, with a streak of big brother in him.

But he wasn't in big-brother mode right now.

Maria scrambled up the last few steps. Michael and Cameron both jerked their heads toward her.

"What's wrong?" Michael demanded. "Did something happen at school?"

"What?" Maria asked. She unsnagged her long skirt from the stair rail. "Oh no. I, uh, I just decided to skip homeroom. No big deal."

They both stared at her. Maria felt a rush of self-consciousness. She clasped her hands in front of her, which made her feel like a little girl getting ready to recite a poem. She linked them behind her. That felt weird, too. She crossed her arms over her chest instead. But wasn't that supposed to be defensive body language? She dropped her arms to her sides and ordered herself to stand still for one minute.

"Michael, I—," she began. Maybe she should have asked to talk to him alone. But it was too late now. "Michael, I—Michael, I—I can't deal with this anymore. . . . I'm going to end up in some kind of asylum if you don't—"

Oh no. What am I saying? *What* am I *saying?* This was worse than anything she'd thought of on the bus. So much worse.

"What are you saying?" Michael asked.

Maria gulped so loudly, she thought it could probably be heard in Texas. "If you don't do what Liz said and choose between me and Isabel."

There. At least she'd said it. Very badly. But it was out there.

"You want me to choose. You want me to choose right now?" Michael asked.

Maria lifted her chin. "Yes. Right now."

She forced herself to look into Michael's gray

eyes. He shot her an angry glare, then looked away. The silence in the room stretched out. He glanced at Cameron.

"Fine, if that's what you want," he finally said. When he looked at Maria again, his eyes were still angry, but there was something else there. Pity? Sorrow? Maria's heart dropped. "Then I'll have to go with neither."

Isabel slid a slice of pizza onto her tray, then added a couple of packets of sugar to put on top. Not that using sugar made the pizza edible. She frowned at the layer of oil congealing on top of the cheddar cheese. The cafeteria's pizza sucked.

Okay, maybe she couldn't expect them to serve brick oven. But would it kill them to lose the left-over spaghetti sauce and try out some mozzarella and basil on a crust that wasn't practically as thick as her binder?

"Excuse me, young lady," a familiar voice drawled behind her. "I was wondering if you would be so generous as to give me a moment of your time? I'm conducting a little survey for my little paper."

Isabel didn't turn around. The last thing she needed today was to have a conversation with that big corn dog Elsevan DuPris. It's true that she got a kick out of his little paper, the *Astral Projector.* She always bought a copy to see if he had another scoop about the bloodsucking alien babies, her faves. But she did not get out a kick out of DuPris.

"Yes, I'm talking to you, young lady, with your hair the color of Dixie sunshine," DuPris continued. He caught up to her and slid her tray out of her hands. "Allow me. Now, here's today's question— would you consider having a child with an alien if you found yourself madly in love with one?"

Isabel felt a cold band wrap around her heart. The buffoon had actually hit on a question she'd done a lot of thinking about. Not whether she'd consider having a child with an alien, but whether a human would ever consider having a child with her. She could possibly want to be a mom. Maybe. Someday.

That's part of what made the idea of being with Michael feel so right. They were the same. He understood her in a way that no human ever would.

"I can see it's a difficult question. You just take your time," DuPris said. He set her tray down in front of the cashier and smoothed out the sleeves of his white suit.

"Actually, it's not difficult at all. I'm not interested in having brats of any kind," she told him. She thrust her money at the cashier, grabbed her tray, and strode off. Fortunately DuPris's southern-gentleman deal meant he would never go chasing after a lady who'd made it clear she wished to be alone. About halfway across the cafeteria she hesitated. She saw Alex, Maria, and Liz at the table they always sat at when it was too cold to eat in the quad. But did she really want to go over to them?

Alex and Maria wouldn't exactly be psyched to see her right now. Still, if she didn't sit with them today, did that mean she didn't sit with them tomorrow? Did it mean she was out of the group?

The group is whoever you're with, Isabel told herself. But she shot another look over at the usual table. Liz, Maria, and Alex were her real friends— as opposed to Corrine Williams, Doug Highsinger, and the other members of the school elite that she used to spend most of her time hanging with.

Even Tish Okabe, Isabel's shopping buddy and loyal follower, didn't come close to being the kind of friend Alex, Liz, and Maria were. That's because the three of them knew the truth about her. They'd been there for her in situations that would have sent anyone else, even Tish, running away at full speed.

That decided it. Isabel took a sharp right and started toward the table.

"I didn't know that Isabel was, you know, interested in Michael," she heard Alex say.

They were talking about her! Isabel turned around and slid in between two guys at the table behind her friends. She flashed an evil look at the loser to her left. She could tell he was about to try to speak to her, and she wanted to hear everything Alex was saying.

"They practically grew up in the same house.

Mr. and Mrs. Evans call him their third child. I've heard them," Alex continued. "I knew Michael and Isabel were close, but I thought it was in *that* way, not in that *other* way."

Poor Alex, Isabel thought, though she was still glad she'd broken up with him. It had to be done. She couldn't keep going out with Alex when every time he kissed her, she ended up thinking about Michael. But she *probably* could have found a gentler way to do it. Make that *definitely*.

Isabel blotted the grease off her pizza, then turned her whole attention back to the conversation going on behind her.

"So what are you saying? You think that Michael's the reason Isabel broke up with me?" Alex asked.

"Her attitude toward you did seem to change after we saw Michael's dream," Maria said reluctantly.

"I don't know if that should make me feel better or worse," Alex said. "I guess it's good to know that she didn't start spending a lot of time with me and then decide that I was worthless scum."

Isabel frowned. She hadn't meant to make Alex feel that way. "No one could ever think you're worthless scum," Liz told him. "It's not possible."

"Yeah, no one could even think you're really valuable scum," Maria added. "You're better than penicillin, even."

"That's mold, not scum," Liz corrected.

"Either way makes me feel better," Alex said.

All three of them laughed, and suddenly Isabel wanted to be over there with them so badly. She grabbed her tray and slowly began to rise to her feet. She didn't want them to catch her at the other table.

"If Isabel's hoping to get Michael now that she du—" Maria stopped midsentence. "Sorry, Alex," she said quickly. "Now that she screwed things up with the best guy in the world, she's dreaming."

Isabel froze. This she absolutely had to hear. She sat back down.

"Michael doesn't want her. Or me," Maria explained, her voice flat. "He wants Cameron. He made that clear when I went to the museum this morning."

Cameron? Isabel thought. The redhead with the buzz cut? Michael must be in post-traumatic shock from the compound.

Well, at least Isabel knew her competition. Neither Maria nor Cameron had a snowball's chance in Hades against her guy-snagging skills. Let the games begin.

Max cracked open the door to Ray's bedroom and did a quick Adam check. He was still asleep, his chest rising and falling so slowly, it was almost frightening. But not as frightening as Adam awake.

He knew Adam was deadly. He'd had firsthand evidence, which was why he still couldn't believe Michael was willing to risk all their lives after he'd seen Adam destroy the compound.

He leaned back his head and rubbed his eyes with the heels of his hands. He felt as if his brain were pulsing, trying to push its way through his skull. The sensation would probably go away if he'd open himself to the collective consciousness. He'd been blocking the knowledge and sensations of the consciousness for days because he'd needed to focus on getting Michael out of the compound.

Well, Michael was out now, so maybe it was time to stop resisting. The consciousness held the knowledge of everyone on his home planet, living or dead. Maybe somewhere there was an answer to what was wrong with Adam, to why he had seemingly gone from innocent to evil in such a short time. Maybe Max could learn how to help him.

If not, maybe he could at least find out if Adam's powers could be stopped. If . . . if he could be killed.

Max pulled a breath deep into his lungs and let it out slowly, relaxing his body, relaxing his mind, allowing himself to connect to the consciousness. Ahhh. It felt so good, so right, like sliding into an ocean exactly the same temperature as his body.

The last time he'd connected to the consciousness, he'd been bombarded by scents, images, tastes, and textures and by information, by a rush of facts that overwhelmed him. Now all he felt was the light brush of many auras against his. The auras, they were what formed his ocean. He could feel them supporting him, lifting him the way a wave lifts a swimmer.

He knew he should try to find a way to search for information about dealing with Adam. And he would. In a minute.

The image of Max breaking free from his incubation pod filled his mind, and an instant later he received a rush of emotion from the others, a mix of joy, and pity, and excitement.

Another image appeared—Max's mother teaching him how to drive. Again he felt the reaction of the others—curiosity about the technology of the car, appreciation of the warmth of the relationship between Max and his mother, wonder that one of theirs could experience this with a human.

He felt as if his essence, his *spirit,* was being discovered and celebrated by all those in the consciousness. The images came faster and faster, with no effort from Max, revealing all the most important moments of his life.

As each image disappeared, Max felt a little piece of his memory fade, dissolving into the ocean of auras. He was becoming part of the whole. The whole was becoming part of him. It was awesome. Transcendent.

The image of his first kiss with Liz exploded in his brain. He felt the others' appreciation of the love between Liz and Max and echoes of the love the others had experienced in their own lives.

Then the memory began to slip away from him, becoming softer and blurrier as it was shared between the billions of entities making up the consciousness.

"Stop!" Max cried. "Don't." He wasn't sure if he was using his throat and tongue and lips to form the words. He wasn't even sure if he was speaking in English. But somehow the others understood him. He felt their bewilderment, their concern.

He couldn't do this. He couldn't share so much with them. If he did, he wouldn't have anything left.

Max used all his will to force the others away from him, to break the connection and stop them from pulling away the memories that formed his own consciousness, that formed the entity called Max.

You're all right, he told himself. You're safe now. You're still *you*.

He opened his eyes, and his heart jackhammered as he saw his own image in the mirror. His body had become almost transparent—like a ghost. He could only see an outline of himself, and his bones and organs were faintly visible underneath.

Max looked down and tried to poke his finger through his midsection. But his finger just jabbed into flesh. He closed his eyes and *squeezed* himself with his mind. He looked back up at the mirror— to see that his body had fully rematerialized.

3

"You might want to move back a little," Cameron warned Michael. "The contents of this Lime Warp soda are under pressure. If I make one wrong move when I open it, that's it. The cap could blow off, causing—" She checked the warning on the side of the can. "Causing eye or other serious injury."

"I'll risk it," Michael answered. He stayed planted on the flat beanbag next to hers.

God, he was sexy. God, she wished he would move just a little farther away. Her whole body was aching for him. But she had to hit the road soon—a couple of days, tops, and starting something with Michael wasn't going to make that any easier.

"Okay, if you want to live dangerously." Cameron unscrewed the bottle top, and the soda gave a gentle fizz. "Kind of anticlimactic," she said. "Like a lot of things."

And you should remember that, she told herself. Yeah, she felt like she'd die if she couldn't feel Michael's hands on her again, but it was probably one of those things that was a lot better in her memory than in reality. Or not.

35

"Oh, really?" Michael asked. "I don't find that at all." He twisted off the top of his soda, and it erupted. That was the only word for it. At least half the bottle spewed up into the air, and the cap hit the ceiling with a pop.

Cameron wiped a little foam off her cheek. "I think you gave that a little help," she accused him.

Michael grinned at her. "All it takes is the right guy."

"Okay, stop," she ordered Michael. "I'm starting to feel like we're in a movie some businessman is watching in a cheap motel."

"That doesn't sound so bad." He leaned toward her, his gray eyes smoldering.

Cameron jerked her soda can up to her mouth and took a long swallow, doing one of those numbers where she pretended she had no idea that Michael had been about to kiss her. She knew what kissing Michael felt like. And she knew if she let herself experience it again, she'd never get her butt out of Roswell.

Runaway rule number one: Always keep moving, she lectured herself. If she stayed here, or anywhere, too long, she put herself at risk of getting caught and shipped back home.

She wished that wasn't true. She wished she could just stay here forever. It was the first place she'd really felt safe in a very long time.

Yeah, safe with the people you betrayed, she

thought. She felt a little sick every time she remembered how she'd manipulated Michael into telling her the names of the other aliens and then told Sheriff Valenti that Max and Isabel were the ones he was looking for.

At least nothing bad had happened to them because of what she'd done. Adam had killed Valenti before he had a chance to do anything with the info. But that didn't change the fact that Cameron had given up Michael's friends just to stop Valenti from turning her over to her parents.

It probably wasn't the last time she'd have to do something like that. That's just the way it had to be. She had to be willing to do anything to survive. It was very nice that Michael had this whole group of people willing to go to the mat for him, but she didn't. She had to take care of herself.

"So, do you want me to help you decide between psycho girl and the cheerleader?" she asked Michael, just in case the move with the soda hadn't discouraged him enough. "Isabel is definitely hotter, but you'd have to be willing to—"

"He's coming out!" Max shouted. A second later Adam burst into the living room, Max right behind him.

Cameron and Michael jumped to their feet. "If you think he's going to hurt you, use your powers on him," he told her, his voice so low, she could hardly hear him.

Oh, good, she thought. Then I'm perfectly safe. I'll just use my powers. The *fake* powers I lied about having so Michael would trust me enough to open up. Sure am glad I have those powers.

Cameron tried to get control over the fear whirlpooling inside her as she looked at Adam. His eyes passed over her briefly as he jerked his head from side to side, scanning the room, but he didn't seem to recognize her at all. She could have been a bug or a piece of furniture.

"What's up, big guy?" Michael called. "Cameron and I were just saying we were in the mood for a card game. Want to play?"

His voice sounded casual and friendly, but he carefully positioned himself between Cameron and Adam, and there was tension in every muscle of his body. Something was obviously very wrong with Adam.

Adam didn't answer. He did another quick survey of the room, then headed straight for the front door.

Michael and Max scrambled around him, blocking his way. "Adam, listen," Max said, his voice soft and gentle, as if he were trying to calm down an animal. "You're sick or something. I know you might not think so, but you are. We need you to stay inside until we find out what's wrong and how to help you."

"Ray took something that didn't belong to him. I have to get it back," Adam answered, his voice deeper than Cameron remembered it. He took a step forward, but Michael and Max wouldn't let him pass.

"Move," Adam demanded.

"No," Michael said firmly. "We're not moving. You want to get past us, you're going to have to take us out. Is that what you want to do, Adam? You want to attack us? Look at us. I'm the one who helped you escape from the compound. Max is the one who took care of you when you got out."

Is he even capable of remembering them? Cameron wondered. He seemed so completely different. Was there enough of the old Adam left to respond to what Michael was saying?

"Maybe you should just let him go," she cried. She'd seen what Adam had done to Valenti. She would go insane if she had to watch that happen to Michael. But there was no way she could fight Adam. She was powerless.

"No, we're not letting him go," Michael answered, his eyes locked on Adam's. "If he wants out, he has to go through us."

Why did he keep saying that? He might as well just dump gas all over himself, hand Adam a blowtorch, and get it over with.

Adam gave a growl of frustration. A tremor raced through his body. Then he collapsed, as if all his bones had turned to liquid.

"This was the first time I've seen him conscious

since we were in the compound together," Michael said. He crouched down beside Adam.

Cameron slowly walked over. She had this crazy fear that Adam would suddenly sit up and attack them all, like a deranged killer in some horror movie. She told herself to get a grip and knelt next to Michael. "The way Adam looks is the only thing that's the same. He was like the world's biggest little boy when he was with us." She gave a choked laugh. "It kind of creeped me out at first, how innocent he was. Like he'd been raised by teddy bears or something."

"Are you starting to understand why I wanted him kept knocked out?" Max asked Michael, his voice cold enough to give a freezer burn.

I thought they were supposed to be best friends, Cameron thought. With friends like that . . . Although she supposed Max had his reasons.

"We're never going to be able to figure out what made him like this if he's unconscious," Michael answered.

"We're never going to be able to figure out what made him like this if we're dead," Max shot back.

"He didn't do anything to hurt us," Michael protested.

"This time." Max shook his head. "What I don't get is why he was talking about Ray. Ray died before Adam got out of the compound."

"I connected to him a few times," Michael said.

"Maybe he got images of Ray from me . . . but that wouldn't explain why he was looking for something of Ray's."

"Well, we can't ask him now." Max bent down and grabbed Adam's limp arms. "Help me get him back to the bedroom."

Michael grabbed Adam's legs and stood up. Cameron stayed where she was, watching as they hauled him off. She hoped Adam stayed out until she was ready to leave. This was a situation she did not need to deal with.

"So is he okay?" she asked when Michael came back into the living room.

He shrugged. "You know everything I know." He dropped back down on the ripped-up beanbag chair he'd been sitting on before Adam's breakout attempt.

Cameron got up and moved over to the de-beaned beanbag chair across from him. It kept her a little farther away from him than before at least. "So are you staying here again tonight?" she asked.

"Yeah. I can't exactly go back to my foster home after disappearing for more than a week," he answered. He flicked some beanbag stuffing off the knee of his jeans. "I guess when this whole Adam thing is . . . over, I'll have to go kiss my social worker's feet. He'll probably have to find me a new home. I don't think the Pascals are going to want me back."

Cameron nodded. She knew how that felt. She doubted her parents had even wanted her on the day she was born. The only reason they wanted her back now was because it seemed the proper parental response to her running away—and because she was a good psychological punching bag.

"So, I was going to help you choose between Maria and Isabel," Cameron said, trying to distract Michael a bit.

"Okay, here's the thing," Michael said. "Say you went into an ice-cream store and the guy behind the counter points to two of the tubs and says you can pick between those two flavors. But the freezer case is filled with all these other tubs with all these other flavors. The two tubs of ice cream look great. You're sure they would taste amazing. But what if you're really in the mood for something else?"

Cameron groaned. "Can we please go back to talking about Lime Warps?" she said, grinning. "Because I have a bad feeling that I'm a tub of ice cream in this scenario. A *tub* of ice cream. Do you notice something about the wording there that might not be overly appealing?"

"Bad scenario. Sorry. Let me try again." Before she knew what he was doing, he had her face cupped in his hands. An instant later his mouth was on hers.

This is a big mistake. This is a monumentally big mistake, Cameron thought. Then she wrapped her arms around his neck and leaned back, pulling Michael down on top of her.

*   *   *

Isabel paused outside the museum's side door and applied a fresh coat of mochaccino lipstick, then she headed in. It was time for her all-night guard duty session. By morning Michael was not even going to remember Cameron's name.

She picked her way across the trashed museum and headed up the staircase leading to Ray's living room. Halfway to the top she heard something that made her blood start to sizzle, something that made it very clear that at least right now, Michael knew Cameron's name very well. He was practically groaning it.

Isabel dashed up the rest of the stairs, and her blood went from sizzling to a full boil when she saw Michael and Cameron sprawled on the floor. Cameron's hands were buried under Michael's shirt. From where Isabel was standing, she couldn't see exactly where Michael's hands were, but she didn't need to see them to know they were someplace they shouldn't be. They should be on her—not Cameron.

She was way prettier than Cameron, no contest. The girl had a body like a boy. Why would Michael want to be making out with that?

They were held prisoner in the compound together, she reminded herself. Maybe that created some kind of twisted thing between them. *Something* must have happened because Isabel was standing about three feet away from Michael and he was so caught up in kissing Cameron that he hadn't noticed. That was just not something that could have happened unless Michael had been through some major psychological trauma.

Well, there was someone who could tell her exactly what went on between them in the compound. And Isabel was going to get the whole story from him right now. She rushed across the room and down the hall to the bedroom where they'd been keeping Adam. Max sat in front of the door.

"Your shift's over," she said. "Liz said to tell you she'd meet you at our house."

"Maybe I should stay," he answered. "Adam . . . it's not that he's done anything, exactly. He only got up once, and Michael and I kept him from leaving, but—"

"Michael's here. We'll be fine," Isabel interrupted. She reached down and hauled her brother to his feet.

"Call me if anything happens," Max told her, his voice tense. "And don't underestimate him, Izzy. You have to think of him as a completely different person from the one we first met. Think of him as dangerous."

"I will. I promise," she answered. Was he ever going to leave? She couldn't talk to Adam until he did.

"Liz and I might go over to Flying Pepperoni, so if you need me and I'm not home, try over there. And if I'm not there, try the Crashdown."

"Flying Pepperoni. Crashdown. Got it," she said. She grabbed his coat from off the floor and thrust it at him.

"Do you have the phone numbers?" he asked as he pulled on the coat.

"There's always information. It's like magic. You call them up, and they'll tell you any number you need to know," Isabel answered. "Now go. Liz is going to be sitting in front of our house, waiting for you."

Max turned around and started down the hall.

Thank you, Liz, Isabel thought.

She forced herself to wait until she was sure Max was out the door, then she slipped into the bedroom and quietly closed the door behind her. Not that Michael and Cameron could hear anything over their own heavy breathing.

Adam lay on the bed, motionless. Yeah, he's real dangerous, Max, she thought. She hurried over and shook him by the shoulder. Nothing. He didn't even flutter an eyelash.

Isabel shook him harder. She wanted to know every single word Michael and Cameron had exchanged in the compound. And she definitely wanted to know if there had been anything physical between them. Anything. If they bumped elbows eating dinner, she wanted to know about it.

"Adam, come on. Wake up." She leaned down until her lips were about an inch away from his ear. "Wake up!"

His eyes began to move back and forth under his closed lids, then slowly they opened. Isabel jerked away. It was an automatic response, like jerking a hand away from a hot stove.

Adam's eyes were . . . People always said eyes were the windows to the soul. If so, Adam looked soulless. They could have been made of glass, like a really fancy doll's.

You're not here to stare into his eyes, Isabel reminded herself. "Adam, tell me everything you know about Cameron," she demanded.

He didn't answer. She wasn't sure he'd even heard her. "This is important. I need to know about Cameron," Isabel repeated. She thought another little shake might get him talking, but now that his eyes were open, somehow she just didn't feel like touching him.

"Come on. We're friends, remember? Friends talk to each other. Tell me about the compound," she coaxed. "Tell me how you met Michael. Tell me something about Cameron. Anything."

A big, fat nothing. That's what she was going to get from him. Isabel stood up. It would have been nice to know exactly what she was dealing with, but it wasn't necessary. The day she couldn't make a guy, any guy, forget about another girl was the day Isabel's coffin slammed shut.

She took a step toward the door, then Adam grabbed her arm. "Oh, so now you're ready to talk." She turned to face him. His blank green eyes stared right through her.

"I don't have time for this," she muttered. She tried to pull her arm away, but Adam tightened his grip, digging his fingers into her bare skin.

And then they were connected. But it wasn't like any connection she'd ever experienced. This was a violation. The images were being ripped from her mind.

She tried to scream, but the muscles in her throat contracted, as if they'd been squeezed by a hand jammed down her mouth.

She had to break the connection. She reached over and slashed the back of Adam's hand with her nails. She could feel warm, slick blood under her fingers, but Adam didn't loosen his hold on her.

She tried to think through the pain tearing through her mind. They were connected. She should be able to feel an artery in Adam's head or his heart and *squeeze* the molecules together until he collapsed or died. She didn't care which.

Isabel used all her will to fight the pain and search for the most vulnerable spot available to her. But she got nothing from Adam. She couldn't even feel his heartbeat or hear him breathing. She wasn't receiving any images from him, even though she could feel him digging through her mind.

There had to be something there. The connection had to go both ways. She squeezed her eyes shut and reached out with her ravaged mind, out and out. Yes. There. Just a little farther.

A flood of images pounded into Isabel. Too many. Too much. Blasting her raw brain.

She opened her lips again. "Michael." She forced the word through her bruised throat. "Michael, please . . ."

Michael unbuttoned another button on Cameron's shirt and discovered a tattoo low on her left shoulder—a hummingbird. He traced one of its wings with his tongue, and Cameron gave out a gasping sigh. She ran her nails lightly across his shoulders, shoving all thoughts out of Michael's brain. He heard a low whimpering sound, and he wasn't even sure if it was coming from him or Cameron.

Then he realized it wasn't coming from either of them. He jerked up his head and listened hard. It was coming from the bedroom, and it sounded like Isabel. He hurled himself to his feet and raced down the hall. He hadn't even realized Isabel was there.

He yanked open the door, and he felt an electric jolt sizzle through his body when he saw Isabel's face contorted in fear and pain. Then he noticed Adam's hand locked on her arm.

Michael gave a growl of fury and grabbed Adam by the back of the shirt. He yanked him away from Isabel and shoved him to the floor, then scooped Isabel up in his arms and laid her on the bed.

"Isabel, I'm sorry. I'm so sorry. I didn't hear you. I didn't know." He brushed her hair away from her face with trembling fingers. "Can you tell me what happened? What did Adam do to you?"

Why was he wasting time talking? He had to heal her. He took a deep breath, getting ready to make the connection, then Isabel reached out and grabbed his hand.

"Not Adam," she whispered, her eyes bright. "I saw . . . for a second I saw . . . not Adam. Something controlling him." Her fingers went limp in his. "It's . . . I saw. Evil."

"You disappeared?" Liz exclaimed. "You must have been terrified."

"Well, I didn't really disappear. I just became kind of see-through. I could see my heart, Liz," Max said.

Liz flashed him a look of horror.

"And guess what? My heart has your name on it," Max said, grinning. As Liz giggled, he slid his fingers through her thick, silky hair, then leaned in for a kiss.

Maybe I should call and check up on the Adam situation. The thought barged into Max's head. He shoved it back out. He wasn't going to waste his Liz time stressing about Adam. Michael and Isabel were with him, and he'd made Isabel swear to let him know if anything strange happened.

He returned all his attention to kissing Liz. Each kiss was a kind of miracle. He'd spent years dreaming about what it would feel like to touch Liz, torturing himself by imagining one perfect kiss over and over. Back then he'd been sure dreams were all he'd ever have. But he was wrong.

51

Liz was right here, sitting next to him on the living-room sofa, her lips a breath away from his. He closed the distance and gave her bottom lip a playful nibble.

Liz pushed him away and shoved one of the big sofa pillows between them. "You stay on your side," she ordered. "No more kissing until we finish talking about the collective consciousness. What do you think would have happened if you hadn't broken away when you did? Would your whole body have disappeared?"

"*Disappeared* is the wrong word to use. The molecules of my body had flown so far apart that it seemed like it was invisible," Max answered.

"When actually it was just scattered in a billion pieces?" Liz asked, her brows drawing together.

"Exactly. Once I realized what happened, I just focused my mind and *squeezed* the molecules back together. It was actually kind of cool." He grabbed the sofa pillow and tossed it across the room. "And that concludes the discussion of the collective consciousness." He looped his fingers around her turquoise necklace and gently pulled her toward him.

"Uh-uh." Liz grabbed another pillow and re-formed the barricade. "Have you thought about the fact that if you'd stayed connected longer, the molecules of your brain could have been separated from each other, too? Then what? How would you have had the capacity to realize anything? How would you have been able to focus and *squeeze* without a mind?"

"I hadn't thought of that," Max admitted. Count on Liz to zero in on the most important piece of information. "I bet it would feel amazing, though. I panicked when my memories started to dissolve into the consciousness. But for the three seconds before I freaked, it was . . . I can't even come up with the right words to describe it."

"Are you going to do it again?" Liz asked.

Was he going to do it again? He had to do it again. Now that he knew it was possible, he couldn't go through the rest of his life without ever allowing himself to experience being part of something monumental, a living entity of cosmic proportions.

Liz wrapped her arms around herself. "You are. I can see it in your face."

He didn't have to ask what she thought. Yellow tendrils of fear were spreading through her aura. A couple of crimson splotches of anger had sprouted, too.

"It's like I've discovered a whole new world, and I have to explore it. The only way I'll really be able to do that is by giving myself over to it, *becoming* it," Max said, struggling to express how he felt about the consciousness.

"Even if it means you won't ever come back to this world? To me?" Liz asked.

Her voice was steady, but he thought he glimpsed the sheen of unshed tears in her eyes. "That would never happen," he promised. "You're what would bring me back. Even if my molecules were spread out from here to whatever galaxy my home planet is in, that wouldn't stop me. All my molecules would be like little homing pigeons. They'd all zoom to you, and then I'd re-form."

"That's very romantic and all, but I don't think there's any scientific basis for your theory," Liz answered. But a few of the crimson splotches disappeared from her aura.

"Wait. I've got it," Max said. "I'll use Michael or Isabel as a spotter the next time. Then if I do disappear completely and have no way of squeezing myself back together, they can do it for me." He ran his hand across the pillow separating them. "Can I get rid of this now? My molecules are really missing your molecules."

Liz snatched up the pillow and tossed it over the back of the sofa. Max didn't need an engraved invitation. He slid his hands along the curve of her waist. He loved the feel of her. Could not get enough.

He was not at all happy to hear the front door open with a bang. He'd been counting on a lot more alone time with Liz. He leaned back and saw Isabel coming down the hall.

"Hey, Izzy, come here a minute," he called. "I want to try something, and I need your help." He turned to Liz. "This way you can be here to see how the molecule thing happens. When Iz helps me re-form, you can tell me how it looked."

Isabel started through the living room without a word. Max reached out and snagged her by the wrist as she passed him. "Come on, it won't take long. I need you to make a connection with me, and—"

Isabel turned to him with piercing eyes and gave him a hard shove. He flew through the air and slammed into the wall next to the fireplace.

Liz rushed over and helped Max to his feet. "Are you okay? What happened?" she asked.

"I'm all right," he answered. He turned to his sister. "Why the hell did you do that?" He and Isabel had had a lot of fights. But they had always had reasons, and Isabel had never been able to physically overwhelm him. Even when she used power.

Isabel didn't answer. She just stared at him, eyes round and blank.

Max strode over to her. "Start talking, Isabel," he ordered.

Isabel gave a breathy squeaking sound. And then she collapsed.

"Help me get her to the sofa," Max called. Liz was at his side in an instant. Gently they carried Isabel around to the sofa and lowered her down.

"Is she unconscious?" Liz asked.

Max knelt next to the sofa and reached for his sister's hand. Before he could touch her, she struggled into a sitting position.

"Maybe you should lie back down," Liz said.

Isabel shook her head. "No, it's okay. I'm okay." She shoved her hair out of her face, then slowly raised her eyes to Max's. "I'm sorry. I can't believe I did that to you. It's just that when you touched me . . ." A shudder swept through Isabel's body.

Liz sat down next to her and wrapped her arm around Isabel's shoulders. Isabel flinched away, but Liz held on tight. "Did something happen at the museum?"

The museum! Max felt like such an idiot. He should have known the second Isabel opened the front door that something was wrong. She wasn't due home until morning. They'd given their parents this whole cover story about how she was spending the night with Maria.

"Was it Adam?" he asked. His rib cage suddenly felt too small, as if the bones were crushing his heart and lungs. "Did something happen with Adam?"

Isabel nodded. "I went in his room to check on

him. He grabbed my arm and made a connection." She stopped and cleared her throat. "It was like my brain was ripping apart." Her aura darkened, a rim of black forming around the outside.

"You're safe now. You're home," Max told her. He knew he should have stayed at the museum. What was he thinking, coming back here for a little make-out session? He stood up. "I'm taking care of this. Adam isn't going to get the chance to hurt anyone else."

"Michael said he was going to put sleeping pills in his food to make sure he stays out. He wants us all to meet tomorrow to figure out what to do now," Isabel said. "But Max, it's not Adam. I've connected with Adam before, and it wasn't him. There's something . . . something. . . ."

Her eyes drifted shut, her breathing becoming slow and even.

"I can't believe it," Max whispered. "She fell asleep."

"How about that girl over by the fountain?" Maria asked.

Alex leaned over the polished metal railing of the mall's upper deck and checked out the girl. Wavy hair that fell almost to her waist, nice waist, nice everything else. "Yeah, she's pretty, I guess," he said.

He realized that somewhere along the line his

way of looking at girls had changed. Now they all fell into two categories—Isabel and not Isabel. That's basically all he saw when he looked at the girl by the fountain. A not Isabel.

"So go talk to her," Maria urged. "Go give her one of your goofy lines. What was that one you told me, something about you have to arrest her for stealing the stars from the sky and putting them in her eyes? She'll love it."

Isabel had loved it. Well, it had made her laugh at least.

"Go on. You can do it. A-lex! A-lex! A-lex!" she chanted.

So she's a not Isabel, he thought. That's what you want. Someone who might treat you slightly better than a human-shaped doormat.

But there was one problem with the not Isabel. She was . . . not Isabel.

Alex shook his head. "I can tell from here that it just wouldn't work," he said. "See that sweeping gesture she's making with her hand? It's obvious that her greatest ambition in life is to be a game show hostess. Which is cool. I mean, who wouldn't want to be a game show hostess, right?"

"Right," Maria answered. "And who wouldn't enjoy talking to a wanna-be game show hostess, if that is what she is? So go."

"The thing is that while most guys would love to talk to a soon-to-be game show hostess, I have this phobia. I don't really like to discuss it, but hey, we're friends, so here's the deal—when I'm in the presence of someone with even the slightest look of a game show hostess about her, I panic. I start trying to buy vowels. I start demanding valuable prizes. And I put everything in the form of a question. It's not pretty."

"Does the word *desensitization* mean anything to you?" Maria asked. "It means gradually exposing yourself to the thing you're afraid of. It's how people get over phobias. Go cure yourself." She tried to push Alex toward the escalator, but he grabbed the railing with both hands and held on tight.

Maria gave a huge sigh. "Fine, forget the elegant hand gesture girl. Amber Whalen's coming out of the card store. Just go say hi."

"Don't know her," Alex answered. But he already knew everything about her. Not Isabel.

"I'll introduce you." She grabbed him by the arm. He tightened his grip on the railing. "You have nothing to be scared of," she insisted. "I don't think she even watches TV. She wants to be a vet."

"A vet!" Alex exclaimed. "I have an even bigger phobia about vets. I can't go near her. Barking would be involved. There would be much humiliation for all three of us."

Maria dropped his arm. "I give up."

"Good." Alex shot her a grin. "Now we can

find someone for you." He pushed himself away from the railing and scanned the upper deck. He wanted to find someone good for Maria. He spotted Josh Martinez wandering in their direction. Excellent choice. "How about Josh?" he asked.

"I like Josh," Maria answered. "Josh is great."

At least this night wasn't going to be a total bust, Alex thought. One of them was going to go home happy. Or at least happier. "So, you want me to stay with you? Or should I take off now so you can talk to him by yourself?"

"Um, you know what, I think Josh is *too* nice. Because he'd be a rebound guy for me. And everyone knows it never works with the rebound guy."

"Everyone knows this?" Alex repeated. "I've never—"

"Girls. Girls know this," Maria explained. "So, anyway, it wouldn't be fair to start something with Josh when it would just crash and burn in approximately eight-point-three days or four dates, whichever came first."

Alex didn't bother picking out someone else for her. He had a feeling no matter who he suggested, all Maria would see was a big not Michael.

"Food court?" he suggested.

"Food court," she agreed.

*   *   *

"How's Isabel doing?" Cameron asked. She lay curled up on a couple of the flattened beanbags, wrapped in one of Ray's *Star Wars* comforters.

"Max said she's still sleeping," Michael answered. He rolled onto his back and stared up at the ceiling. It wasn't nearly time for his two hours of sleep yet, but he was keeping Cameron company until she dozed off.

"So she's okay," Cameron said.

"No thanks to me," Michael muttered. "If I'd listened to Max in the first place, Adam would never have had the chance to even put a finger on Izzy."

"Is that Max talking or you?" Cameron asked.

"Both, I guess," Michael admitted. "Let's just say he wasn't happy about what happened." He didn't even want to think about their conversation. They'd ripped into each other pretty good, and they never did that. It had always been him and Max against—

Cut it out, Michael ordered himself. In another second he'd be in the middle of some chick flick moment. A montage of his and Max's most special moments. Max pushing Michael into a pile of leaves. Michael cheering Max up after he struck out during the big game.

"Is Adam . . . ?"

Cameron's question pulled him away from his thoughts. "Our boy Adam is still circling the airport, and I'm making sure he stays that way," he assured her.

"What do you think Isabel meant when she said there was something evil controlling him?"

Michael shook his head. "No clue. I'd almost be happy if she was right, though. At least it would mean I wasn't totally deluded about Adam."

Cameron mumbled something that sounded like an agreement. She was close enough that he could hear each breath she took. And the scent of her, that clean ocean smell, was driving him nuts. He wanted to reach over and pull her up against him. And why shouldn't he? A couple of hours ago they'd been all over each other.

But it felt different now. A lot had happened. Plus it was night, and they were going to spend that night sleeping in the same room. Which made the stakes a little higher. Like if he touched her now, she could think he was looking for more than he actually was. At least more than he actually was tonight.

"So, uh, I saw the hummingbird tattoo. Got any more?" he asked. He figured the way she answered might tell him if she was thinking about the same thing he was thinking about or if she was just thinking about sleep.

"There's one more. I never let anyone see it, though," she answered.

That didn't sound like an invitation. But it

wasn't a slap, either. Michael turned onto his side so he could look at her. It was hard to read her expression in the dim light coming from the hall, hard to see her aura, too. "No one's seen it? So, where is it?"

Cameron laughed. "I can hear the drool dribbling out of your mouth," she teased. "Suck it in. The tattoo's on my ankle. The reason I never let anyone see it is it came out really ugly. It's supposed to be a dragon, but it looks more like a mutant piglet. I'm going to get laser surgery done when I get the cash together."

"I could do it right now," Michael offered. "All I have to do is connect with you, then push the molecules of ink out of your skin."

"No, that's okay," she said quickly. She rolled onto her other side and made a big production out of fluffing her pillow and adjusting her blanket.

Nothing hard to read about those signals. "Are you afraid?" he asked harshly. "What, do you think if I connect with you, I'll hurt you, the way Adam did Isabel?"

"It's not that." She sat up and flicked on the light switch.

"So?" He sat up, too.

"So, it's just not a good idea, all right?" she said.

Michael couldn't stop himself from checking

out the long stretch of bare leg the T-shirt Cameron was using for a nightgown showed off. "Not a good idea," he repeated. He didn't get it. Touching her in any form seemed like a great idea.

"I probably should have told you this before, but I'm leaving town tomorrow," she announced.

Just like that. Michael thought back to himself sitting in his cell in the compound, parceling out the women in his life—Cameron, Maria, and Isabel. He wasn't sure why, but Cameron seemed to be the one—the one he could potentially love. But not if she just up and left.

"No biggie," Michael muttered.

"It's not safe for me to stay in one place too long. Especially a small town," Cameron went on. "Strangers get noticed."

Michael felt some of the muscles in his shoulders loosen up. This was something he could fix. All he had to do was rearrange some molecules, and he could give Cameron a whole new face. He could change her appearance every single day if that's what it took to keep her around.

"Let me show you something." He leaned over and touched her face. He made the connection almost instantly. Images from Cameron flickered through his mind.

A little girl Cameron fighting not to cry as a woman vigorously brushed Cameron's long red hair. A mirrored tray covered with perfume bottles. A worn paperback book—*The Little Princess*. An older Cameron leaping over a track hurdle. A needle injecting ink into skin. Cameron standing next to Sheriff Valenti, watching Michael and Adam through a two-way mirror. A varsity jacket.

Cameron yanked Michael's hand off her, breaking the connection. "I just told you not to do that," she ordered him, her voice low and angry. "Don't go pawing through my mind."

"Afraid of what I'll see?" Michael asked. Why was Cameron in an observation room with Valenti? She was a test subject. She should have been on the other side of that two-way glass. Was she some kind of informant for Valenti? Michael felt his face reddening.

"Ever hear of a thing called privacy?" she demanded. "What made you think—"

"What exactly was the deal between you and Valenti?" Michael interrupted.

"I told you. I agreed to let him test my powers so he wouldn't turn me over to my parents," she answered, her brown eyes locked on his face.

Liar, he thought. She was trying way too hard to look him in the eye.

He felt his stomach churn with a cold, oily liquid as he suddenly remembered something Max had told him. Max had said that Valenti already knew that he and Isabel were aliens when they showed up at the compound to break Michael out.

Michael hadn't thought all that much about it. It hadn't turned out to be much of a problem since Adam fried the sheriff about two seconds after the words had come out of his mouth.

"You were in Valenti's office when Adam killed him, weren't you?" Michael asked slowly. "I mean, you said you saw it happen, right?"

The color drained from Cameron's face. She knows exactly why I'm asking, Michael realized. Some of the acid from his stomach rose up into his throat.

"Yeah. I was there," Cameron answered.

"You were there because you'd just told Valenti what you found out from me. You told him that Max and Isabel were the other aliens." It wasn't a question.

"I don't have any powers," Cameron admitted. "Valenti said if I didn't get him the information he wanted, he'd take me back home personally."

Michael nodded. He couldn't even look at her. She'd played him for a chump.

"I didn't know you then," she said.

He didn't answer.

"Michael, come on, I didn't even know you then," Cameron repeated.

He still didn't answer. He couldn't.

"Fine. You want it this way, fine," Cameron finally said. "I'm out of here."

Liz snuggled into bed. Her thoughts went from Max's kiss, to Isabel's odd fight with Max, to Max's kiss again . . . until she gently faded into sleep.

"I need to talk to you, Liz," a voice whispered. "It's important. Please wake up."

Liz forced open her eyes, and she felt her heart give an erratic flutter. Adam was sitting on the side of her bed.

Don't let him know that you're afraid, she instructed herself. Just listen to what he has to say, and maybe he'll leave.

"Do you remember when I picked you flowers?" he asked.

Liz nodded. All she could hope was that Mama and Papa wouldn't hear a guy's voice coming from her bedroom in the middle of the night. If they did, they'd be in here in half a second. And Liz was very afraid Adam would hurt them.

"I remember," she said.

Adam smiled his sweet, shy-little-boy smile. Liz forced herself to smile back, her top lip sticking to her teeth because it was so dry.

Now what? Adam wasn't saying anything else. He was just staring at her with his bright green eyes. She noticed that his gaze kept flicking to her mouth. Was he thinking about kissing her? She couldn't let that happen. He could make the connection with the slightest bit of contact and do to her what he'd done to Isabel.

"I'm really cold. I need to put on, uh, more clothes," Liz mumbled. As she stepped from her bed to the floor, she gasped. Her floor was soft, and patches of color had appeared before her eyes. A waft of pollen filled the air, and Liz realized her room had been transformed into a vibrant flower garden. Reds and lavenders, chrysanthemums and roses, all resting on a soft bed of mossy grass. She looked at Adam in astonishment.

"I need to tell you—something important. But I need you to trust me first. I thought it would help if you could remember something good about me," he explained. "That night it was good, wasn't it?" He smiled again, in a serious way this time. "Even though you did say that Max was the only one who could touch you."

"I'm ready to hear what you have to say," Liz answered, relieved to hear that her voice sounded steady. The flowers were comforting, but she was still suspicious of Adam.

He nodded nervously. "You're in danger. All of you. There's something inside me. It's—"

A hideous gagging sound spewed from his throat. He bent over, hacking and choking.

Liz scrambled over the bed to his side. "Adam, what's wrong? What's happening to you?"

He straightened up, and she could see that his face had taken on a faint bluish tint. "Inside . . . inside."

He gave a deep, ragged cough. Liz screamed as he lunged forward and landed on the bed, then began to writhe with seizures.

"You don't need to be here. I told you, I'm keeping Adam knocked out," Michael told Max.

Obviously Max didn't trust him. Obviously he planned to spend the day watching Michael watch Adam.

"I'm not staying," Max answered. "I thought you might be hungry." He thrust a white paper bag into Michael's hands.

Michael opened the top, and the smell of fresh crullers hit his nose. He peeked inside. Max, Mr. Reliable, had remembered the hot sauce.

"Uh, thanks," Michael mumbled.

"I hope Cameron likes crullers, too," Max said. "I didn't think about getting something else so she'd have a choice."

Michael snagged the *Star Wars* comforter off the living-room floor, rolled it up, and tossed it into the corner. "She says she's taking off, anyway. She doesn't like to stay in one place too long."

"Hmmm." Michael caught a flash of concern in Max's eyes, but Max didn't push for details.

"You were right about Adam," Michael said,

doing a fast subject change. Not that the new subject was anything he really wanted to talk about, either, but he knew he had to bite the bullet. "What you said on the phone last night was true. What happened to Isabel was my fault."

Max shook his head. "I was out of line," he answered. "All you did was take a shot on someone you thought you could trust. It's not like I've never done it. When I told Liz the truth about us, I didn't listen to your warning signals."

"That turned out fine. Good, even," Michael said.

"It could have gone the other way, though," Max countered.

"You want a cruller?" Michael asked. He was ready to end this little discussion. If he'd just screwed up on the Adam call, it would be bad enough. But Cameron had been strike two. He'd actually believed he could trust her.

Max pulled a cruller out of the bag. "I'm not eating any of that hot sauce."

He and Michael flopped down on the floor and attacked the bakery bag.

"Hey, before I leave, you want to help me with something?" Max mumbled through a big wad of cruller. "I think if I let myself connect with the consciousness, I can spread all my molecules out so far I disappear and then re-form them. I think. But since my brain could disappear, too, maybe not.

Maybe it won't occur to me—or what used to be me—to rematerialize. Does that make sense? I figured you could help bring me back if there's trouble."

"Do you think we could re-form you in a different place?" Michael asked.

Max shrugged. "Maybe."

Michael snorted so hard, he could feel hot sauce stinging the inside of his nose. "Now you're really going to be king of the science fiction geeks. No contest. You've got to let me hear you say it. Just once," he begged.

"What are you talking about? Say what?"

"Beam me up, Scotty." Michael laughed, spraying little cruller bits onto the front of Max's shirt.

"I haven't watched that show in a long time," Max protested.

Michael wiped his mouth with his sleeve. "So you want to do it right now?"

"Yeah. Let's make the connection." Max grabbed Michael's wrist. "Don't leave me hanging out there."

"I've got you covered," Michael answered. Then his mind was filled with images from Max. The pictures flew past faster and faster until the last one shattered in a rain of sparks that dazzled Michael's eyes.

When his vision cleared, he saw that Max's right arm had disappeared to his shoulder. His shirtsleeve hung limp and empty.

Would the connection hold when Max didn't have a body for Michael to touch? They hadn't even thought of that.

Michael closed his eyes again and focused his mind on Max's body, on *their* body. He could hear Max's heart beating along with his own, feel Max's breath in his own lungs.

Yeah, this should be okay. With the connection it was like he and Max shared a double body. So when Max was *gone,* the Michael part of their body would still be here to re-form him.

Unless because of the connection Michael's body flew apart, too. Something else they hadn't thought about.

Michael heard one of their hearts stop. He felt a chill rush through him. Max's heart was gone. He opened his eyes and saw Max's eyes staring back at him.

Only his eyes.

An instant later they disappeared, too.

Time to bring him back. Michael focused on Max's molecules. He could feel them all around him. But there were so many of them, an almost infinite number.

A wave of dizziness swept through him. Where was he supposed to start? Yeah, he could squeeze some of the molecules together, but which ones? It's not like they were spread out in exactly the right groups, waiting for Michael to put Max back together like some preschooler's puzzle where the head goes up there and the feet go down there.

Michael shoved his hands through his hair and tried to deepen his concentration. But he had no clue which of the billions of molecules came from Max's brain tissue and which came from the muscle of his heart.

Why didn't Max think of this? Max's whole reason for existence was thinking of things like this. He was always so careful, so logical. Why did he have to choose now to experiment with recklessness? Couldn't he have just squeezed a toothpaste tube from the middle or something?

You said you would bring him back, so bring him back, Michael ordered himself.

He ignored the molecules and concentrated on Max. Just Max. He felt sweat breaking out on his forehead and dripping down his back as he concentrated on willing Max to re-form in front of him.

He sensed some movement in the molecules but didn't allow himself to get distracted. He kept one hundred percent of his focus on Max. A network of lines began to form a few feet away, starting about six feet in the air and ending on the ground.

Not lines, veins and arteries. Michael could see the blood pumping through them. He could feel it pumping through *him*. The connection with Max was unbroken.

A pocket of air darkened and began to pulse, and Max's heart slowly re-formed. Max's other organs reappeared much faster, almost too fast for Michael to take it in—lungs, liver, pancreas, stomach, intestines, brain.

Michael felt Max join the effort to pull his molecules together, and bone and muscle appeared, weaving around the organs. The changes happened so quickly, Max's body began to blur. And then he was complete except for his eye sockets. They were empty, blank and staring.

"You're giving me the wiggins, Max," Michael muttered. And Max's blue eyes reappeared, gleaming with excitement.

"That was too cool," Max cried, just as the cow clock in Ray's kitchen started to moo. "I've got to leave," he added. "I don't want to be late for homeroom." He started for the door.

"Uh, Max, just a suggestion," Michael said. "Before you go, you might want to put on some clothes."

"What?" Max slapped his hands onto his bare chest. "Oh. Whoa. Maybe next time I can figure out how to take some molecules of clothes with me." He bolted over to the pile of clothes on the floor and yanked them on. "See you later. We're all heading over right after school to decide what to do about Adam."

Max started toward the door again, then turned around and headed back to Michael. "There's one more thing I want to say to you, something I should have said the day we all made it out of the compound alive," Max told him. He gave a loud sniffle and wiped an imaginary tear off his cheek but couldn't hide his grin. "I love you, man."

Michael laughed. "You're sick—you know that, don't you?"

Max clapped him on the shoulder. "Yeah," he said. "But I like it that way."

Liz checked the bulletin board, then pushed her way back out of the crowd surrounding it. She almost slammed into Maria.

"I knew you'd be here," Maria said. "I don't know why you're so obsessive about the class standings. Every month you're number one. Every month you will continue to be—" She stopped herself. "Wait. Why are you so pale? You *are* number one, aren't you? Arlene Bluth didn't knock you out of first place, did she?"

"No, I still rule," Liz joked.

"Then what's wrong? I know something is," Maria insisted, stretching out one of her blond curls and letting it boing back into place.

"Did you see the bulletin board?" Alex interrupted as he raced up behind them.

"Yep, we're standing next to the class valedictorian," Maria answered. "There's no way it's not going to happen."

"I'm not talking about that," Alex burst out. "Although congratulations and everything," he added to Liz. "I'm talking about the flyer next to the class standings list. The flyer announcing the ROTC program starting at our happy little school. My weasel brothers did it. They managed to talk Principal Shaffer into sending in the application. I am so doomed."

"Do you absolutely have to join?" Maria asked.

"Oh no, I guess not." Alex slapped his forehead. "What was I thinking? I don't have to join. I can just change my name and go live in Siberia."

"Why Siberia?" Liz asked. She understood why he didn't think he'd be able to hold out against his the-military-is-life dad.

"You've got a point," Alex shot back. "Siberia's probably not remote enough." He gave a drawn-out groan of frustration. "Maybe it won't be too bad. Maybe I'll meet some GI Jane kind of girl. That could make it worthwhile, although I don't know if I could be with someone who has better abs than mine." He pushed open one of the cafeteria's double doors and held it open for them.

"Look at those biceps. Whoo, baby," Maria joked as she passed him.

"Are you okay?" he asked Liz as she

headed through the door. "You seem kind of . . . something."

"I just had a bad dream," Liz answered.

"Liz, you should tell us what it was about," Maria said over her shoulder. "It will help get it out of your system. I know, we can help you make up a new ending. That's how you're supposed to get rid of bad dreams—you make up new endings for them and poof, they're gone."

Liz slid onto the bench at their usual table. Alex and Maria sat across from her. "It was about Adam," she told them. "He said we were all in danger. He said there was something inside him, but before he could say what, his tongue fell out. Then his whole face started coming apart. A piece of his cheek plopped onto my arm. That's when I woke up."

She could almost feel the piece of flesh against her skin right now. Moist and meaty. She decided to leave her lunch in her backpack.

"So how would you want the dream to end?" Maria asked. "Actually, you can change more than the ending. You can change the whole thing. Like you can make Adam someone other than Adam."

"Wait. Are you sure it was a dream?" Alex interrupted. "I mean, do you think Adam could have used his dream-walking power to try and communicate with you?"

"I thought of that," Liz answered. "I'm not sure, but it felt like Adam, the real Adam. He wanted to tell me something. He wanted to give us all some kind of warning."

Alex's green eyes darkened. "Maybe that *something inside him* found a way to stop him before he could."

Isabel handed her dad's credit card to the Victoria's Secret saleslady. She already had on her new purchase—a silky, pale pink camisole edged with a thin row of delicate lace. Only the tiniest peek of it was visible under the V neck of her sweater. Just how she wanted it.

When she showed up at the museum, she didn't want to look like she was on some kind of manhunt. That kind of desperation was so not Isabel. No, she didn't want to look like she'd put any special thought into what she was wearing at all. What she did want was for Michael to catch a flash of the camisole and be . . . intrigued.

The saleslady handed the card back, Isabel signed the slip, and she was out of there. She strolled to the mall exit, not breaking a sweat, and then made her way across the parking lot and over to the bus stop. Usually she would have at least tried to con Max out of the Jeep keys, but he would have totally freaked if he knew she was planning to go out of the house. He thought she was spending the day in bed, recovering.

"Isabel, I thought you'd still be home in bed," Michael exclaimed. He ran over to the staircase and watched her climb up the last couple of steps. "Are you sure you're feeling okay? Maybe you should have skipped the meeting."

"What meeting?" she asked.

"Everyone's coming over after school to figure out the Adam deal," he explained. "They should be here in about an hour."

"Oh, right," she mumbled.

"Sit down, at least." He snatched up three of the beanbags and stacked them.

"Michael, I'm fine. Relax, okay?" She dropped to the floor, and he positioned himself across from her. "Actually, I hardly remember any of what even happened yesterday. Max had to explain everything to me when I woke up."

"Whoa. Well, that's good, I guess." He wondered if her mind had blocked out what she'd seen when she connected to Adam because it had been too disturbing for her to handle. He would never forget the expression of raw terror on her face when he burst into the room.

"So, where's Cameron?" Isabel asked.

Michael was glad he couldn't see the expression

on his own face when he heard that question. He wished he could record an answer and play it for everyone who asked.

"She took off," he muttered. "Didn't think Roswell was safe for her anymore."

"What? She just took off? I thought you guys had a little something goin' on," Isabel said.

Michael raised an eyebrow at Isabel, then smiled. "Well, we don't have anything now."

Isabel started playing with the neck of her sweater, and he caught a glimpse of some kind of silky thing underneath. He realized his eyes had lingered there a little too long, and he forced them up to Isabel's face. She was staring at him, an unreadable expression in her eyes.

"What?" he asked.

She raised an eyebrow. "What, what?"

"You were staring at me," he answered.

"I like being able to look at you," she answered. "I thought I was going crazy when you were in the compound. I kept thinking I might never see you again." She paused and pulled in a shaky breath.

"I knew you guys would find a way to get me out of there," he answered.

"I could feel you all the time—you know, feel your feelings," she continued. "Whatever I was doing, it's like you were with me."

Including when I had my tongue in Cameron's

mouth? he thought. An echo of that sensation hit him so hard, he could almost taste her again. He slapped the memory away.

Michael knew Isabel was waiting for some kind of response. This time he had no idea what to say, so he just nodded. Like a big jerk.

"So, you know Alex and I broke up, right?" she asked.

And Isabel takes the gloves off, he thought. "Yeah. I heard."

"Michael, I saw your dream," Isabel blurted out. "You had your arms around me. So now you can't . . . Why are you acting like you have no feelings at all for me?"

"What dream?" he asked, picking the easier of the two questions.

"The *dream*," Isabel repeated, as if that cleared everything up. "It was a little while before you got captured. Maria and I decided to go dream walking just for fun. She picked your dream orb, and we saw you holding me."

"Wait a second here," he said, a smile of recognition spreading across his face. "Isabel, I think you misinterpreted that hug. It was actually part of a nightmare. I dreamed that Max died and we were at his funeral. That's why I was hugging you."

"Oh," Isabel said. Her face reddened as she looked at the ground.

"It's not that—" Michael struggled to find the right words. "It's just that you're my Izzy lizard," he said, using the pet name he'd come up with for her when she was a little girl.

"And that's it?" she asked. "You've never thought of me any other way?"

"Okay, yeah, I have," he answered. He was a guy. He'd thought about a lot of things with a lot of girls.

But it was different with Isabel. He didn't think about her in that fast, speculative, pretty much automatic way he thought about a cute girl in the park or whatever.

"I've definitely thought about you as something different from a big brother," she confessed. "We come from the same place. We understand each other in ways that no human could understand us. That means something."

It meant a lot. Isabel would never betray him. It would be like betraying herself. Maybe she was right. Maybe they were capable of something more.

Michael's eyes locked with Isabel's, and when she leaned toward him and found his lips with her own, he didn't pull away. They kissed—a deep, full kiss.

But there was nothing there—no chemistry whatsoever. It was like kissing his little sister.

Michael started to pull back, but Isabel laced

her hands behind his neck, keeping their lips pressed together.

Suddenly an ice pick of pain stabbed into Michael's brain. He tried to jerk away, but Isabel's hands were now pressing firmly on his back.

Michael made one last attempt to get free before his vision dimmed. His world went black.

Cameron did a quick study of the people scattered around the tiny bus station. Yeah, there were a few good faces. She should have no problem scoring a ticket.

She headed up to the window, scanned the departure times and the rates, and picked a town that was twelve bucks away. Twelve bucks was an amount that a kind stranger would be willing to give to a girl in need.

"One for Hobbs," she told the ticket guy. She reached into her pocket and allowed a slight frown to cross her face. Nothing major. She checked the other pocket. She felt her stomach cramp, as if she'd actually expected to find something there and was sort of sickened when she didn't.

I should be one of those method actors, she thought. The ones who totally live the parts they play.

"Something wrong?" the ticket guy asked.

"My wallet's gone," she answered, the tiniest quaver infecting her voice. "I know I had it at breakfast." She checked her pockets again. "Is the three-fifteen the only bus to Hobbs?"

"Only one today," he answered.

"I really have to get home today. If I called my dad, could he use his credit card to pay for the ticket?" Cameron asked. "I could call collect."

"That would be fine," the guy answered. Not a trace of suspicion on his face.

Damn, I'm good, she thought as he slid the phone toward her. She punched in the numbers for a collect call, then the numbers for a pay phone in front of a deserted gas station she'd stumbled across three towns ago. She'd been using it as hers ever since. If she happened to get picked up by the cops, she liked being able to give them a number where she was sure it would ring and very sure no one would answer.

Cameron held the receiver tight to her ear. She knew that made her look really tense. She gave the ticket guy an apologetic smile. "Just let me let it ring a few more times," she whispered. He nodded, giving her a sympathetic smile back.

Milk it just a little longer, she coached herself. She counted five more rings, then reluctantly hung up. "I guess he's not home. He works out of the house, so he should be there, but—"

Cameron shot a glance at the clock, then she leaned toward the ticket guy. "Um, is the bus station open all night?" she asked, keeping her voice soft, but not so soft the audience behind her in the waiting area couldn't hear.

88

"Only until six," he answered.

"Oh. Okay." Cameron felt her pockets one more time, then turned and headed to the door. She'd figured out that's how it worked best. No begging. No sob stories. She let the little fishes come to her.

"Excuse me, miss?" a voice called just as Cameron's fingers snagged the door handle. She turned around, a who-me expression on her face.

A middle-aged woman gestured her over. "Why don't you let me loan you money for the ticket?"

"Are you sure?" Cameron asked, widening her brown eyes as if she just could not believe this was happening.

The maternal-looking woman opened her purse, counted out the bills, and pressed them into Cameron's hand.

"Oh, thank you so much," Cameron said graciously. "Please, write down your address so I can send you the money when I get home."

The woman dug out a scrap of paper and a pen and wrote down her address. Cameron made a big show of carefully placing it in her pocket. Then she did everything short of grabbing the woman and kissing her. Why not? She deserved to feel good for her twelve bucks.

And maybe someday Cameron would send her the money back. Cameron had a list of all the people she'd promised to mail money to. If she ever got settled someplace and got a job, she would pay it all back.

With one last smile over her shoulder at the woman, Cameron rushed up to the ticket window. She bought her ticket and headed straight to the bus. It was more than half empty, so she had no problem finding a seat to herself.

In less than ten minutes they should be moving out. She couldn't wait. With the exception of Michael, Roswell had nothing but bad memories. She focused her gaze on the back of the seat in front of her, trying to imagine that the bus was already on the road. Someone had graffitied a heart and dagger on the thick plastic. Cameron reached out and traced the design with her finger.

The memory of Michael's mouth tracing the hummingbird on her shoulder hit her so hard, she almost gasped. She could practically feel the warmth of his lips.

She dropped her head back on the torn seat cushion and gave a muffled groan. In some ways it was one of her worst Roswell memories because it was always going to be linked to the memory of the shattered look on Michael's face when he realized she'd betrayed him.

Maybe someday, when she was, like, forty, scientists would figure out a way to do memory surgery, where they just burned out any piece of brain that held a bad memory. She'd be the first in line. Maybe they could even let her keep the hummingbird memory and destroy the shattered look memory.

She snorted. Even if the technology did get developed, it's not like it would work for her. If all her bad memories were lasered out of her brain, she wouldn't have enough gray matter left to operate a can opener, which meant the image of Michael's disappointed face would be etched in her head for the rest of her life.

The driver climbed on the bus and started collecting the tickets.

The conversation with Michael began replaying in her head. She didn't want it to, but she couldn't stop it. She listened to herself explaining why she'd given Valenti Max's and Isabel's names. Why hadn't she apologized?

Too late now, she thought. She pulled her ticket out of her pocket. Besides, an apology wouldn't make him stop hating her.

The driver reached for Cameron's ticket. She didn't let it go. "I forgot something," she blurted out. She bolted out of her seat, stumbled down the narrow aisle, flew down the steps, and hit the parking lot running.

It was a couple of miles to the museum, and there was probably a bus that went there, but

Cameron didn't want to waste time trying to find it. She wanted to get to Michael, spit out her apology, then exchange her ticket and finally get out of this town.

A few blocks later she reached the main street. She hung a left and kept running. It was a straight shot to the museum now. She pushed herself hard, almost glad when her lungs started to burn. It distracted her a little from what she was about to do.

When she reached the museum, she darted around to the side door and pushed through without breaking her stride. She raced to the staircase and went straight up.

She found Michael lying on the living-room floor. Her heart constricted at the sight of him.

He's asleep, she thought. But there was something about the slackness of his mouth and the absolute stillness of his body that told her she was wrong.

Cameron stared at him for a long moment, unable to move. She realized that Michael's eyes weren't completely closed. She could see a sliver of white beneath the lids. She moved her gaze down to his chest. Was he even breathing? She couldn't tell.

She slowly approached him and poked his shoulder with her toe. "Michael! Wake up!" she shouted, her voice coming out weirdly high and breathy.

He didn't even twitch.

"Michael!" she shrieked. She jammed her toe into his shoulder. His body slid a few inches but remained still.

She knelt down, drew in a shaky breath, and lightly pressed her fingertips against the base of his neck.

She didn't feel a pulse.

Maybe it was just too weak to feel. She lowered her head and pressed her ear against his chest.

She didn't hear a heartbeat.

She squeezed her eyes shut and listened harder. She heard a pounding sound, and for one exhilarating second she was sure he was alive. Then she realized the sound was coming from the stairs. She shoved herself to her feet just as Max appeared, with Liz right behind him.

"I think Michael's dead," Cameron cried.

Max shoved his way past her and took Michael's head in his hands. He closed his eyes and started taking deep, even breaths.

Cameron turned to Liz. "Can they bring back the dead?" she asked urgently. "Is that one of their powers?"

Liz shook her head, her eyes on Max and Michael. Cameron locked her teeth together. She was afraid if she tried to ask another question, even say another word, she might start screaming and never stop. Her jaw muscles began to ache as she stood there, waiting, watching.

Michael's left foot gave a jerk, then his eyelids snapped open. He stared up into Max's face. "Prince Charming, I've been waiting for you for so long," he muttered.

A hoarse laugh burst from Cameron's mouth, and the tension in her muscles eased up.

Max didn't answer Michael. He jumped up, strode down the hall to the bedroom, and flung open the door. "Adam's gone," he announced as he hurried back over to Michael.

"Where's Isabel?" Michael demanded, shoving himself to his feet.

"She stayed home sick," Max reminded him.

"No. She was here. We were kissing. That's the last thing I remember," Michael shot back.

Max and Liz ran toward the kitchen. Michael rushed to the bathroom. Cameron stayed where she was. Kissing, she thought. Michael and Isabel were kissing.

"Adam must have knocked you out and taken Izzy with him," Max said when he, Liz, and Michael had returned to the living room.

"Why are you so sure it was Adam?" Cameron asked.

"Michael's brain stem had been pulverized from the inside," Max explained. "Only another one of us could have done that."

"With the sleeping pills I gave him, I can't believe he even managed to roll over." Michael pulled a medicine bottle out of his pocket and checked the dosage instructions.

"Maybe he didn't do it," Cameron said. "Maybe Isabel did. Do you think she could have carried Adam out of here on her own?"

Michael whipped his head toward her, and Cameron felt scalded by his gaze. "Isabel would not do this," he said, his voice low and deadly. "Everyone is not like you."

It was as if the floor had been yanked out from under her feet. "How can you even compare—," she began. Then she stopped herself. She couldn't have this conversation. Not right now, at least. Not in front of Max and Liz.

"Cameron may be right," Max said.

"I don't believe you," Michael exploded. "How can you say that about your own sister?"

"No, listen." Max shot a glance at Liz, and she gave him a quick nod. "Yesterday Isabel used her powers to slam me up against a wall. She apologized, said she was freaked about what happened with Adam, but . . ."

Michael shoved his fingers through his hair. "Isabel said there was something evil in Adam, something controlling him," he muttered to himself.

"What if she was right?" Liz asked. "Could whatever it is be in Isabel now?"

Cameron was very glad Liz had asked that

95

question. It was something Michael needed to think about, but if Cameron had been the one to say it, he would have totally gone off.

"We have to at least consider it as a possibility," Max answered. "Fact—Isabel's not here. Fact—she never would have left Michael to die of her own free will. So either Adam regained consciousness, attacked Michael, and forced Isabel to go with him—"

"Or something evil has control of Isabel," Michael finished.

"Okay, we checked the mall. We checked cheer-leading practice. Now where—UFOnics?" Alex asked.

"It's sort of early for that," Maria said. "Besides, it's in the part of town Michael and Cameron are searching."

Michael and Cameron. Would she ever get used to saying that? Would she have to? Max had told Liz that Cameron was gone. But no.

"How about Flying Pepperoni?" Alex pulled off his sunglasses and tossed them on the dashboard.

"I guess," Maria answered. "It seems kind of hopeless, though. Unless the evil thing in Isabel has some kind of pizza craving."

Neither of them said a word for a long moment. Maria could feel the silence building up inside her, pushing at the walls of her body.

"Are we having fun yet?" Alex blurted out, a wide, maniacal grin breaking across his face.

"Oh yeah," Maria answered. "We're having more fun than—more fun than—"

"Than the last pancake at a breakfast buffet?" Alex suggested.

Maria squinched up her nose. "I have no idea what that means."

"Yeah, me neither," Alex admitted.

Silence filled the car again. Maria felt like a balloon that was about to pop.

"Did I used to have a life?" she suddenly exclaimed. "I mean, what did I do when I wasn't doing this?" She made a helpless swirling gesture with her hands.

Alex laughed. "You mean before the alien invasion? You were enjoying your glory days, gathering up the memories you would come to treasure in your old age."

He sounded so . . . bitter. Maria twisted the silver ring on her pinkie around and around. "Can I ask you a horrible question?"

"Uh, sure," he answered.

"Do you wish that we didn't know the truth about Michael and Max and Isabel?" It was something she'd been asking herself a lot lately.

Alex hesitated. "It would be easier . . . ," he finally said.

That was true. A lot easier. Not just because

alien bounty hunters and evil controlling things would no longer be a part of her world, but because there would be no one she loved so hard, it hurt. There would be no Michael.

"But no," Alex concluded. He shot a glance at Maria. "What about you? Do you wish you could go back in time to before it happened?"

Back to a time when her heart had never been broken. Back to a time when she had never kissed Michael, never told him she loved him.

Maria let out a long, sighing breath. "No. I don't want to go back."

"Look, you said you had something to say to me. We've been driving around for more than an hour and nothing," Michael burst out. "I'm giving you three more minutes. That's it."

He couldn't stand having her in the car another second, her with her ocean smell. Even all those pine tree air fresheners Ray had looped around the rearview mirror couldn't completely block it out.

"Why three more minutes? How did you come to that random decision?" Cameron protested.

Now she was getting attitude.

"Three minutes because that's how long it takes to get to the bus stop from here," Michael answered. "You want to spend your three minutes on stupid questions, go ahead. Talk about the weather for all I care. But that's all you're getting." He didn't know why he was giving her that much.

"I don't know how to say what I want to say," she admitted.

"Three minutes," he warned her. "Less than that now."

She rubbed one finger over her lips, then started talking. "About what happened with Valenti . . . I'm sorry. I—"

"Don't bother," Michael interrupted. He tightened his grip on the wheel until his knuckles went white. "I don't need to hear any more lies."

"I'm not—"

Michael interrupted her again. "You said you didn't know me. That was your excuse, right? You didn't know me?"

"Yeah. I swear, if I'd known you, I never—"

"See, a lie. You didn't know me when you made your little deal with Valenti, I'll give you that. But you knew me when you got Max's and Isabel's names out of me. You sure knew me when you gave their names to Valenti."

He shot a glance at her. She looked stunned. "You actually believed your own lie, didn't you? You actually managed to convince yourself that you never could have done what you did if you'd known the people you were hurting. Well, that's bull. You knew, and you didn't care."

That hurt. He could see it in her face. Good. If

he had to face the truth about her, she would have to face it about herself. Why should he be the only one with his guts torn out?

She turned away from him and stared out the window. "By the time I got to know you, I was already in the compound. I was trapped."

"What, and I was there for some kind of all-expenses-paid vacation?" he shot back. "We got Adam out. We would have found a way to get out ourselves sooner or later. But you had to take the easy way."

"Easy, yeah," she muttered sarcastically. "Everything's easy for me."

"Oh, right, I forgot. You have some bad situation at home. And that makes everything you do okay." Michael sped up and made a left turn with a squeal of tires. He shoved the gas pedal down harder, made another screeching turn. He wanted her out of this car now.

"Here's the bus station. Have a nice life." Michael jerked the car to a stop, reached over, and pushed open Cameron's door.

"I'm sorry," she mumbled one more time. Then she jumped out and raced across the parking lot.

Michael watched her for about two seconds, then he slammed out of the car. "Cameron, wait," he shouted. She didn't turn around, but she stopped. He rushed up to her, grabbed her by the shoulders, and forced her to face him. She wanted him to apologize. It was written all over her face. But Michael couldn't let it affect him.

"I'm sure somewhere along the road, you're going to need money," he said. "And you'll probably start thinking that if you just told the right people where they could find some real, live aliens, you'd be all set. But I promise you this, you ever say a word about us to anyone, and I will hunt you down and kill you."

Cameron's skin paled as her face went slack. For once she didn't toss out a canned comeback, and Michael knew his message had hit home. He turned on his heel and walked away without so much as a backward glance.

"The cave is a great hiding place," Max said. "If Isabel managed to escape from Adam—or break free from something controlling her—that's where she'd go. She feels safe there."

"That makes sense," Liz agreed. She climbed out of the Jeep and helped Max cover it with the tan tarp he used as camouflage when he parked in the desert.

"Ready?" Max asked.

Liz nodded, and they started their hike to the crack in the desert floor leading to the cave. The sun was beginning to set, painting the mountains and pillars of clouds gold and pink. Looking at those clouds, Liz found it hard to believe that evil existed anywhere.

But that was a sentimental thought. Foolish. No, more than that—dangerous. Refusing to believe that evil existed made it almost impossible to fight.

Max reached out and took her hand. His touch comforted her, reminding her that at least she wouldn't have to fight alone. His grip tightened when they neared the cave's entrance, and she realized that he was drawing strength from her, too.

"Let's just hope she's there," he said, then he released her hand and swung himself down into the cave. Liz scrambled after him, finding the big rock with her toes and jumping from there.

When she landed, it took Liz a moment to process what she saw. Isabel and Adam lay on the cave floor—and they both looked *green*. Someone stood over them, cackling. When the man turned around and faced them, Liz's mind reeled.

It was Elsevan DuPris—and he had the Stone of Midnight in his hand.

DuPris smiled at Max. "I've been looking for this for more than fifty years," he said, without a trace of his southern accent. "Who knew that your sister held the information I needed locked inside her little pinhead? Her memories led me right to the spot where you had hidden the Stone."

"Who are you?" Liz whispered. She felt as if her world had been turned inside out. She had spoken to this man so many times during her life and had always dismissed him as a harmless wacko.

"My guess is . . . he's not human," Max said.

"Very good," DuPris answered.

"And if he's not human, then he must be the . . . stowaway Ray told us about," Max answered, his voice shaking with anger. "The one who stole the Stone of Midnight and hid on board my parents' ship."

Liz let her eyes slide over him. Even the way he held himself was different now. He'd been walking around Roswell for years, letting everyone think he was a UFO-obsessed nut job. That took incredible patience, she realized. He must have wanted the Stone very badly.

Max took a step toward him. "The Stone doesn't belong to you."

Liz wanted to reach out and yank Max back to her side. Why was he challenging DuPris? Didn't Max know that all they could do right now was try to get themselves and Isabel and Adam out of the cave alive?

"Finders keepers, isn't that what they say here?" DuPris tossed the ring into the air and caught it, then slid it onto his finger. "I have plans for this. I could use some help, if you're interested. If you're not interested, well, help doesn't always have to be voluntary, if you know what I mean." He pointed his palm at Isabel and

Adam. On cue, they opened their eyes and rose to their feet.

Liz forced herself to stare into Isabel's blank eyes, then Adam's. Izzy's eyes looked like they had yesterday when she had shoved Max against the wall. A rush of understanding swept through Liz. Had DuPris been controlling people from afar? Was he controlling Isabel when she shoved Max? Was he behind Adam killing Valenti—and that rabbit? Was there a way for Liz to help them break free of DuPris's control?

"What do you say, Max?" DuPris asked. "I can't offer you a partnership, but there is room for advancement in my enterprise."

Say yes, Liz thought. Say what you have to say to get us out of here. This wasn't the time to fight. They needed time to find the others and make a plan.

"*You* crashed that ship!" Max cried. "*You* killed my parents!"

"Don't take it personally," DuPris answered, strolling toward them. "They were going to take me back to our planet for judgment. I had no choice."

Liz saw Max's hands curl into fists. She knew he was going to launch himself at DuPris any second. She grabbed his arm. "Remember the compound, Max. Adam was being controlled by *him*." She jerked her chin toward DuPris. "It was *his* power that killed Valenti and started the fire."

104

"You understand me," DuPris told Liz. "I could use a girl like you, a human girl. I suspect that you would be easier to keep in line than those two." He gestured at Isabel and Adam. "They managed to slip away from me a few times before I got a firm enough grasp. But you, I'd like to see what I could do with you."

Quick as a snake striking, he grabbed Liz's wrist. "No!" she screamed.

Liz's scream echoed endlessly through the cave. The sound paralyzed Max, freezing his muscles. He had to get between DuPris and Liz, but he couldn't move.

No, that wasn't true. He could move—he *was* moving—turning toward DuPris, but so slowly, it was almost impossible to perceive. Liz and DuPris— they were caught in the same phenomenon. Liz's mouth was still open in the same scream. DuPris hadn't tightened his grasp on her wrist.

Max felt a drop of sweat begin to trickle down his cheek, slowly . . . absurdly slowly. Time, he thought. The movement of time has been altered.

At least his mind hadn't been affected. At least he had the ability to realize what had happened. Was slowing down time something DuPris had done to stop Max from interfering? Had DuPris already made a connection to Liz? If his brain was working as quickly as Max's, DuPris could be turning her into his puppet right now.

Max couldn't take this. It was making him insane.

Liz was right next to him, and he couldn't do anything to help her.

Pressure began to build up behind his eyes, penetrating deep into his brain. He knew that sensation. It came from the collective consciousness, a call for him to connect.

He continued his minuscule movements toward DuPris, the drop of sweat maddening him as it slid another fraction of an inch. Maybe he should connect to the consciousness. Maybe then he'd find a way to manipulate time himself. He concentrated and soon felt himself expand outward—beyond the cave, beyond the realms of Earth.

This time there was no warm ocean of auras waiting to embrace Max. He felt as if he'd been hurled into the core of a volcano, lava boiling around him. Every being in the consciousness was seething with hatred and fury, all directed at Elsevan DuPris. They spewed out emotions they had been holding in for all the years since he escaped from their planet.

Traitor, they called him, although not in words but in rushes of jagged feeling that Max felt in his blood and bones. Traitor. Liar. Thief. Every being joined in the chant. Betrayer. Soulless. Murderer.

Max's mouth stretched open, and a howl of rage escaped, the beings of the consciousness using his voice as their own. Time rushed forward, and instantly Max was in the air, throwing himself at DuPris.

As soon as they hit the cave floor, Max rammed his fist into DuPris's abdomen. His hand sank in so deep that he could feel DuPris's stomach under his fingers. A wave of revulsion swept through him. DuPris's body was as soft as clay—or else connecting to the consciousness had given Max incredible strength.

A burst of power struck Max's temple, but it was as soft as a cotton ball. He had the strength of millions, DuPris the strength of one.

Pain. The consciousness wanted the traitor to feel pain. Suddenly Dupris's face twisted in agonized terror and Max could see inside him. He could see DuPris's insides being ripped apart, could feel DuPris's organs moving beneath his fingers.

Liz let out a long, shrill scream. Max felt like screaming, too. What was he doing? It took every ounce of his strength, but somehow Max pulled his hand away from Dupris's convulsing form. Immediately DuPris started to heal. Max could feel him growing stronger.

"Nooo!" the beings of the consciousness roared.

Max again had no control. He reached in, holding both hands over DuPris's heart. "You're killing him!" he heard Liz scream.

He knew it was true, but he couldn't stop. He was an instrument of the consciousness.

Please, no, he silently begged. He used all his will to squeeze his eyes shut, but he couldn't stop himself from feeling DuPris's heart beneath the skin, fighting against him. Pounding, then slowing, then slamming, then stopping.

"Max! Max!" Liz shrieked his name again and again, her voice vibrating with terror.

He couldn't answer. Dizziness and nausea swirled inside him. He felt as if the cave floor were spinning beneath him. When would it end? When would they let him stop?

He felt his eyelids twitch. He fought to keep them shut as the spinning sensation intensified, but a moment later they sprang open, DuPris's body becoming just a blur of color. "The Stone, the Stone, the Stone, the Stone," the beings of the consciousness shrieked.

Max could see a speck of purplish green in the blur. His hands jerked out. They came back with the ring—and DuPris's finger.

"Do you want some antistress tea?" Maria asked. "After that, I think you could definitely use some antistress tea." She got up and rushed to the stove. "Oh, and thanks for meeting here. My mom has a date, one of those critical third dates, and it's not like she'll ever hire a baby-sitter for Kevin as long as I'm alive because it's not like I have a life."

Michael wished he could reach over and grab

her and pull her down on the chair next to him. She was so clearly terrified by Liz's description of what had happened in the cave, and he had this tremendous urge to just hold her and try to make it better somehow. But he and Maria were in a place where holding her would only make things worse.

Maria pulled in a gasping breath. "Baby-sitting. Yeah, that's a very big problem," she rushed on. "Why don't we discuss that? Hey, I know, maybe we could form a club. A baby-sitters club. That would be something fun for us all to do together."

"Let me help you," Alex said. He jumped up and took the teapot out of Maria's trembling hands.

Michael saw him whisper something in her ear, something that helped her get a grip. He looked away, forcing his attention back to Liz. "So when Max passed out, DuPris just took off?"

Liz nodded. "He used Adam and Isabel to help him out of the cave."

"One of them's probably already healed him," Alex said.

"Yeah," Max agreed.

Michael whipped his head toward the kitchen door and saw his friend slumped against the door frame. "You shouldn't have gotten up," he said. Max looked horrible. His skin had a grayish tint, and there was a strange *withered* spot on his throat.

"Had to," Max answered. He crossed the kitchen and dropped down into the chair next to Michael's.

"We were just about to come up with a plan to deal with DuPris," Alex told him. He started setting down mugs of tea on the table. "Liz . . . got us up to speed."

Michael was glad that Max hadn't had to relive what had happened. He knew Max had to be torturing himself for what he'd done. That's how he'd think of it—what *he'd* done.

Michael wasn't looking forward to the day when he went through his *akino* and made his own connection to the collective consciousness. They'd used Max like a puppet today. It didn't seem all that different from the way DuPris was using Isabel and Adam.

"I know what I need to do to deal with DuPris," Max said. "I got instructions, actually more like a blast of knowledge, from the consciousness before the connection broke." He looped his fingers around the handle of the mug and turned the mug in a slow circle. "Do you know what a wormhole is?" he finally asked.

"There's a theory that says that the gravity of black holes pulls on more than just the objects around it, that it actually pulls on space and time, and that it can create a tear in the time-space continuum. A wormhole is the passageway made by the tear," Liz answered.

"You forget who you're talking to here," Alex told her.

"It's a shortcut through space," Liz said.

"And if I channel the energy of the consciousness, I can create one," Max explained. "After I do, I'm supposed to use it to send DuPris back to our home planet."

"There's only one problem," Michael said. "We have no idea where DuPris is. He could be anywhere. He, Isabel, and Adam could have left town. Or they could all have different faces and be hanging out at the mall."

"Did Isabel . . . was she okay when you saw her?" Alex asked Liz.

"Yeah. I don't think DuPris will hurt her or Adam," she told him. "It doesn't make sense—they're like his slaves. He wants them around."

"Anyone have any ideas about how to track them?" Alex asked. "Max, is that anything the collective consciousness could help with? Do they know where DuPris is?"

Max shook his head. "Today in the cave it was the first time anyone on our home planet had seen him in more than fifty years. They had no idea where he was. He's not connected to them. I don't think they have any way of sensing his movements."

"I'm almost surprised they want you to send him back," Liz said softly. She lowered her head, her hair falling forward and hiding her face. "I'm

113

surprised they don't just want you to kill him. It seems like what they wanted in the cave."

Michael didn't think Max would have been able to live with himself if the consciousness had succeeded. If his hands had been used to kill someone, even someone as evil as DuPris, it would haunt Max every day for the rest of his life.

"Seeing him practically made them insane," Max explained. "But now . . ." He gave a hoarse laugh. "I don't know—I guess they cooled down. They want to put him through some kind of judgment."

"I have an idea," Maria said suddenly. She'd never rejoined the group. She stood over by the sink, twisting a dish towel in her hands. "Liz, you said that Adam came into your dream and tried to tell you who was controlling him, before he started convulsing. Anyway, it seems like DuPris figured out he had to stop Adam from, uh, making outgoing calls. But maybe he forgot that there could be incoming calls, too."

"So I should go into Isabel's dream and ask her where DuPris took her and Adam when they left the cave," Michael said, feeling a tinge of hope. "Great idea."

"Thanks," Maria mumbled, without looking at him.

"I'll try it right now. Isabel could be taking a beauty nap at any point." Michael closed his eyes and tried to let his mind go blank. Thoughts kept

114

bombarding him. What was going to happen to Isabel and Adam if he couldn't do this? How did Max get that withered spot on his neck? Was it dangerous?

As soon as he shoved one thought away, another one replaced it. Could the wormhole take Michael back to their home planet, too? Did he want to go? Were he and Maria ever going to be able to just hang again? And what was DuPris making Isabel and Adam do right now? And—

Michael felt a light, tentative touch on his shoulder. He opened his eyes and saw Maria standing next to him. "You're never going to be able to focus in here. Come on."

She turned and headed out of the kitchen. He stood up and followed her as she led the way across the living room and down the hall to her bedroom. He reached for the light switch, but Maria grabbed his hand.

"Leave it off. It will make it easier for you to relax," she said, then she seemed to realize she was still holding his hand and dropped it fast. "Now take off your shoes and lie down."

Michael kicked off his sneakers and stretched out on the bed. He felt a little of the tension ease out of him. Maria's room was one of his favorite places.

"Okay, I know you think aromatherapy is a big joke, but smell this, anyway." Maria thrust a little vial at him, and he obediently took a sniff. He would have done pretty much anything she told him to right then. She seemed a lot less freaked now that she was all caught up in her healing arts stuff—that's what she called it, healing arts—and if doing this was helping her feel less afraid, that was all he needed to know.

"Really breathe it in," Maria instructed.

The lilac scent made the inside of his nose burn, but he didn't tell her that. He just pulled in a lungful of the stuff.

"Now close your eyes," she said, her voice soft and almost musical.

It's got to work this time, Michael thought as he shut them. If it didn't, Isabel—

He felt Maria's hand smoothing out the wrinkles the thought had made in his forehead. "Focus on the lavender."

He found himself focusing more on the scent of *her*. Had he totally screwed things up with her? Could they ever just be couch potatoes on this bed again, watching a triple feature of old horror movies? And what was that withered spot on Max's neck?

Maria started rubbing her fingers in little circles on Michael's temples. "You can't stop thinking, can you? Okay, here's what I'll do. I'll talk to you. Listen to me instead of your thoughts," she said. "Mozart used to have his wife read to him when he was composing because it got rid of the chatter in his

116

head and let him concentrate. If it worked for Mozart, it can work for you."

The warmth of Maria's fingers felt as if it were seeping deep into Michael's brain. He settled deeper into her bed.

"Lavender used to be my favorite color in the box of sixty-four crayons—you know, the one with the sharpener built into the side," Maria said, her voice calm and sweet. "It seemed like it could draw anything. It was the right color for everything. I drew lavender flowers and my father's lavender eyes, my mother's lavender smile. They were the same to me, mother, father, flowers. All good. All lavender. And I was lavender, too."

Michael's breathing slowed down. The thoughts that had been attacking him faded into a babble that was easier for him to ignore.

"We were made up of the same stuff," Maria continued. "The boundaries warm and fuzzy. Mom was me, and I was Dad, and he was all of us and the flowers. My father used to hang the pictures I drew up on the refrigerator before he . . . before he left. He said I'd created a beautiful world, a beautiful lavender world."

Maria's voice faded as the spinning orbs of the dream plane became visible. He was in. He turned in a slow circle, his eyes darting over the glistening iridescent orbs as he searched for Isabel's.

He didn't see it. But that didn't mean it wasn't

there. Michael began to whistle, calling to Isabel's orb. Maybe she wasn't asleep right now, although Adam had slept pretty much nonstop. Or was that even sleep? It was more like unconsciousness. Could Isabel even dream?

Adam got to Liz, he reminded himself. He continued to whistle. He'd stay in the dream plane all night if he had to. It was their only shot.

He sat down, and one of the orbs circled around his head, playfully brushing his cheek. Michael knew that orb. He'd visited it quite a few times when he was about thirteen and obsessed with Patrice Burgess, the woman who worked in the dry cleaners near foster home number whatever.

Michael nudged Patrice's dream orb away. A few seconds later he felt a light brush on the back of his neck. Take the hint already, he thought. He turned to flick it off and saw Isabel's orb hovering behind him.

He held out his hands, and her orb spun into them. He peered inside and saw a blond doll in a bikini driving a little pink convertible. The car kept zooming halfway up a steep hill, then rolling back down.

Where was Isabel? He didn't see her anywhere.

Doesn't matter, he told himself. He'd just expand the dream orb, then go inside and find her. He began to whistle again, slowly moving his hands apart, urging the orb to grow.

It began to shrink instead. This had never

118

happened before. The orb had been the size of a volleyball, and it had already shrunk down to grapefruit size. There was no way he could get inside.

"Isabel," he shouted. "Where are you?"

The doll in the convertible turned her head. It's Izzy, he thought. He should have realized it before. Isabel was dreaming she was the doll.

With a sucking sound the dream orb collapsed to the size of a baseball. Before Michael could react, it was the size of a golf ball.

"Izzy, you have to tell me where you are," he screamed. "Where did DuPris take you?"

Michael heard another sucking sound. The orb was going to shrink again. "Tell me!" he cried.

"Cameron knows," Isabel wailed, her voice like a squeaky hinge.

What? Had Cameron betrayed them again? Was she working with DuPris all along? "What do you mean? How does she know?" Michael yelled.

Before Isabel could answer, her dream orb shrank to the size of a marble, then to the size of a pea, and with a tiny pop, it disappeared altogether.

8

"The ticket guy remembered Cameron," Michael announced. He swung himself back behind the wheel of the Jeep. "She traded in a ticket to Hobbs for one to Albuquerque. That bus left more than two hours ago, but it makes a couple of stops, including the airport, which eats up some time. If we really motor, we should just be able to beat it to the station."

Was this the hand of fate trying to bring Cameron and Michael together? Maria wondered as Michael wheeled the Jeep around and sped out of the parking lot. Maybe the two of them were destined to be a couple. Maybe Maria should be really happy for them because they'd found their soul mates.

Maybe she should ask Michael to pull over so she could puke.

You shouldn't even be thinking about that stuff, she told herself. You should be thinking about Isabel and Adam. She managed to concentrate on sending them some positive thoughts for about two seconds before she started wondering why Cameron had left town in the first place. Did she and Michael

121

have some kind of fight? Would they end up doing the whole joyful I-was-wrong-no-no-I-was-wrong thing at the bus station? Would she have to watch them kiss?

"Next time you work at the Crashdown, I'm sure my papa is going to ask you how you did on your life science test, okay, Maria?" Liz asked. "I told him you needed me for an all-night study session tonight or you'd flunk it."

Maria could hear the tension in her friend's voice. Maybe Michael would have to stop the car for her, too. Liz was always so careful to be the most perfect daughter. She wasn't as skilled as most about lying to her parents.

"Got it. I'll tell him that I never would have passed if not for your brilliant tutoring," Maria promised. "I hope the baby-sitter remembers the cover story I told her to give my mom." She gave a choked half laugh. "Actually, it probably doesn't matter. My mom's so in lust, she probably won't even notice that the baby-sitter isn't me."

Alex groaned. *"Mom. Lust.* 'One of these words is not like the others. One of these words just doesn't belong.'"

"Tell me about it," Maria answered. "New subject, please."

"I have one," Alex said. "What I don't get is how Cameron could know where DuPris took Isabel and Adam."

Cameron wasn't exactly the new subject Maria had been hoping for. But what did it matter? Whether they talked about her or not, Maria would be thinking about her. She couldn't help herself.

"And if Cameron saw them, she wouldn't have just gotten on a bus," Liz added. "She would have stayed in town until she found you and told you, right, Michael?"

"Look, there's something you have to know about Cameron," Michael said, his eyes locked on the road. "Everything I told you about her was a lie, and that's because everything she told me about herself was a lie." He rushed on. "She wasn't in the compound as a test subject—she was in there as a spy for Valenti."

"Spying on you?" Maria asked softly.

"Got it in one," Michael answered. "Valenti promised her if she got the names of the other aliens in Roswell from me, he wouldn't turn her back over to her parents."

He shot a glance at Max over his shoulder. "I told her." He spat out the words as if they tasted bitter on his tongue. "I betrayed you and Isabel."

Maria could imagine what had happened. Michael had believed Cameron was a prisoner, just like him. He saw the two of them as united against Valenti and the Project Clean Slate people. Why wouldn't he tell her the truth? She opened her mouth, wishing she could say something to comfort him, but she couldn't find the words.

"Cut yourself some slack," Alex told Michael. "She already knew the truth about you. It's not like you were telling her that there were aliens on Earth."

"And she helped Adam escape," Liz added. "Why wouldn't you trust her?"

It didn't matter what the rest of them thought, Maria realized. What would matter to Michael was what Max thought. She turned and looked at him. He still seemed totally wiped out.

"You didn't betray me," Max said. "Cameron betrayed you."

The tight, guarded expression on Michael's face didn't convince Maria that he believed Max.

"So what do you think Cameron's deal is in this situation?" Alex asked. "Why do you think she didn't say something if she knew where DuPris took Isabel and Adam? She can't have any connection to DuPris, can she?"

"Don't ask me," Michael answered. "It's not like I have a great track record knowing what's really going on with Cameron. I'm the one who told her—"

"Don't even go there again," Max interrupted. "Cameron betrayed you. End of story."

End of story for Max, Maria thought. But Cameron had torn something deep inside Michael. Even when it healed, there would probably always be a nasty scar.

Kind of like the one she had. Kind of like the

one Alex had. Didn't anybody's love story get a happy ending?

She took another glance over her shoulder. Oh, right. Princess Liz and Prince Max.

Liz stared up at the sky as the Jeep sped down the long, straight stretch of highway to Albuquerque.

"Looking for binary pairs?" Max asked softly.

She hadn't been, but she said yes, anyway, remembering a night not too long ago when she and Max had sat in the parked Jeep, talking about the future, looking up at the star-filled sky. That night she had told Max that the two of them were like a binary pair, two stars so close together, they appeared to shine the same light. That had been the night Max had finally agreed they could be more than just friends, a night she'd never forget.

As if he could read her thoughts, Max reached over and took her hand.

Liz felt a little shiver whisk along her spine. She couldn't shake the image of that hand, Max's hand, covered in gore. Clawing open DuPris's body cavity.

"Max, do you trust the collective consciousness?" The question burst out of her.

"I don't know what you mean," he answered, his voice flat.

"I know what she means," Alex jumped in. "She means totally without your permission—no, more than that, totally against your will—the consciousness used you to try and kill someone. Not exactly a trust builder."

"I explained to you that the beings in the consciousness were furious. Basically they just lost it when they saw DuPris," Max said. His grip on Liz's hand tightened.

"And that's okay with you?" Michael demanded. "Because you had your *akino* and joined them, they can just make you do whatever they want whenever?"

Liz was glad to hear that she wasn't the only one who had some doubts about the consciousness. Hopefully hearing concerns from all of them would get Max thinking.

"Not whenever," Max protested. "It was just that one time."

He didn't answer Michael's first question, Liz noted. She knew the answer, anyway. What the consciousness had done to Max was not okay with him.

She twisted her hair into a knot on the top of her head, something that always helped her think better. And something that gave her a reason to slip her hand away from Max's.

"It's already turning out to be more than one time," she finally said, working to keep her tone gentle. "Now they've ordered you to open the wormhole and send DuPris back."

"Ray Iburg is part of the consciousness. My parents are part of the consciousness. You don't think that's enough of a reason to trust it?" Max exclaimed.

Ah, there it was, Liz thought. The reason Max wasn't letting himself acknowledge that he hated what the consciousness had done to him.

"There are millions of beings in the consciousness, though, right?" Maria asked tentatively. "So what Ray or your parents want, that might not be what the consciousness makes you do."

"They aren't making me do anything," Max snapped.

Michael snorted. "Tell that to DuPris," he muttered under his breath.

Max wrapped his arm around Liz and pulled her closer against him. The wrinkled spot on his neck brushed against her cheek. She twisted around and ran her fingers over the patch of skin. It felt dry and hard, mummified. "Do you know what did this to you?" she asked. She was almost positive she knew the answer, but she wanted to hear what Max would say.

"Huh-uh," he answered. Liz felt like shaking him. She would have if she thought it would do any good.

"I know I'm not a science geek like the two of you," Alex said, leaning across Liz to check out Max's neck. "But even to me it seems significant that it appeared right after the consciousness had control of Max."

"I guess," Max mumbled.

"When they had control, it drained you," Liz

127

said, deciding to spell it out for him since he didn't seem capable of analyzing the situation on his own. "You're still exhausted. What I want to know is—" She pulled in a deep breath. "What's going to happen to you when you open that wormhole? How much is that going to take out of you? Are you going to end up like this all over your body?" She flicked the wrinkled spot. "Are you . . . are you going to die?"

Max didn't answer, but Liz felt the tension filling his muscles.

"Didn't the consciousness bother to tell you what could happen?" Michael demanded.

"The knowledge I received—" Max stopped abruptly and turned his head away from Liz, peering out into the desert whizzing by.

"The knowledge you received," Alex prompted.

Liz felt as if all the air was being sucked out of her lungs as she waited for Max to reply.

"It will take a lot of strength, from me and the consciousness. There's a . . . possibility it could take too much out of me for me to recover," Max admitted. "But I have no choice. DuPris is evil— none of you are going to try to argue with that, I hope—and I can't just let him wander around making the world his own private puppet show."

Michael slammed his foot on the brake, and the Jeep squealed to a halt. He jerked around to face Max. "When were you going to tell us this?" he yelled. "What am I saying? You weren't. You were just going to be Saint Max and die for the good of humanity without a word of complaint."

"I'm not planning to die," Max yelled back.

Liz struggled to pull in a breath. Her lungs felt flat and useless, as if her chest had gotten too tight for them to expand. "Maybe there are other ways to deal with DuPris," she said.

"Ways where no one ends up dead," Maria added.

"Let's talk about it on the way to the bus station," Alex instructed. "No matter what we decide to do about DuPris, we've got to find Isabel and Adam."

Michael turned back around, and the Jeep jolted back down the highway. "We could just kill DuPris," he told them. "I had a problem with the consciousness using Max to do it against his will, but I have no problem with going in there and doing it myself."

"That's crap," Max shot back.

Liz agreed. She could see Michael killing if he had no choice, if there was no other way to save an innocent life. But it wasn't something he would do casually.

"I don't know if you could kill him if you wanted to—no offense," Alex added. "It was DuPris's power combined with Adam's that turned Valenti into the Abominable Ashman, remember?"

"Too bad we can't use the ring," Maria said. "The Stone of Midnight might be strong enough to send

DuPris back without using any of Max's power."

"If we knew how to work it." Liz loosened her hair and immediately reknotted it.

"And if it didn't send a signal to the bounty hunters that would not die," Michael added. "I thought I killed one of them, and it just divided into two parts. Both alive."

"Hold the phone!" Alex exclaimed.

"Hold the phone?" Michael repeated. "What are you, a dork?"

"A dork who's going to save Max's smooth pink butt," Alex answered. "The bounty hunters were hired by the beings on your home planet because they wanted DuPris brought back for judgment. Let them do their job."

Suddenly Liz felt as if she could breathe again—deep, full breaths of the cold night air. "So we give DuPris the ring. He won't attack because Max almost killed him the last time."

"I don't think I could do it again even if I wanted to," Max said. "I would need the strength of the consciousness, and they don't want him dead anymore."

"We have to pray DuPris doesn't know that," Liz said. "So anyway, we give him the ring."

"We tell him it's in exchange for Adam and Isabel so he won't get suspicious," Maria suggested.

"And then we stand back, way back," Alex concluded. He gave a couple of little bows. "Thank you, thank you."

"So what do you think, Max?" Liz asked, feeling her chest start to tighten up again when she saw the somber expression on his face.

"I think it could work," Max said. "But if it doesn't . . ."

He let his words trail off, but Liz knew what he'd planned to say. If their plan didn't work, Max would open up the wormhole. Even if it killed him.

"Wait here," Michael ordered as he pulled up in front of the Albuquerque bus station. He leaped out of the Jeep and raced inside. "Did the bus from Roswell come in yet?" he called to the woman behind the ticket counter.

"That's it out there," she answered. She pointed out the back window at a bus. An empty bus.

"Did the people already get off?" he demanded.

She blew a big bubble, and Michael got a whiff of grape gum and garlic. "Do you see anyone on it?"

He rushed up to the counter. "When did it get in?" he asked.

"Not more than a few minutes ago." She blew another bubble, this one so big, it obscured half her face. Michael resisted the urge to reach out and pop it.

"Did you see a girl get off?" He was talking so fast, his words were tumbling out on top of each other. He forced himself to slow down. "She's tall, about five-ten, thin, short red hair?"

"Answers to the name of Cameron?" a voice asked from behind him.

He spun to face her.

"If you decided to give me another thirty seconds, forget about it," she told him. "I have nothing else I want to say to you." She started toward the door.

Michael lurched forward and blocked her, grabbing her by the shoulders. "Where is she?"

Cameron tried to pull away, but he tightened his grip. He was not going to let her go until she'd told him everything. She jerked up her head and stared him right in the eye. "Where is who?"

Truly an excellent liar, Michael thought. "Isabel. And Adam. You know where DuPris took them."

"Last time I saw them was in the museum with you, okay? Now let go, or—"

"Or what?" Michael interrupted. "Or you'll find the Albuquerque sheriff and turn me in?"

Her eyes darkened, and he felt the fight go out of her. She stood there passively, no longer trying to get free of him. "If I knew where they were, I would tell you," she said. "I would do anything I could to try and make up for . . . I just don't know. I don't."

Michael started to shove her away, then he saw something that made him tighten his grip until Cameron winced. "You don't know where they are," he repeated. "Then you want to explain to me where you got Isabel's necklace?"

Cameron's hand flew to her throat. "A little girl dropped this in my lap as she was getting off the bus."

"Is there some kind of problem?" the woman behind the counter asked, cracking her gum.

"No," Cameron answered.

She could have said yes. She could have tried to get him booted out of there. But she didn't.

Michael released her. "A little girl? Was she alone?"

"She was with a guy in his twenties, her dad, I thought. There was a little boy with them, too." Her eyes widened. "Do you think it was *them?* You think DuPris changed their appearance?"

"I think it's possible." Thank God, Isabel had found a way to drop him a clue. "Where did they get off? What stop?"

"It wasn't one of the scheduled ones," Cameron explained. "They got off near this old ranch house in the desert. The bus driver didn't want to stop. It was kind of an issue."

"Can you show me?" he asked.

Cameron nodded.

"It's over there. See it?" Cameron pointed to the left and Max could just make out the moon-lit shadow of a low ranch house in the near distance.

"Should I drive right up?" Michael asked.

"Why not? We're just here to make a little trade. We come in peace, right?" Alex said.

133

"I think that's supposed to be my line, earthling," Michael told him.

Max ignored them. He was trying to get ready for *whatever* he was going to have to do in there.

"You okay?" Liz asked him.

He nodded without looking at her. Looking at Liz was the last thing he needed right now. If he had to open the wormhole, he might never see her again. For him death didn't mean obliteration. He knew that now. If he had to . . . make the sacrifice, he'd join the others of the consciousness, join Ray and his parents, live on as part of the billions.

But he'd never be able to touch Liz again. Never be able to smell her hair. Never be able to see that dimple that appeared and disappeared in her left cheek. What else was death but losing all that?

Maybe the plan will work, he told himself as Michael pulled up in front of the house.

"Is there anything you want me to do?" Cameron asked.

"Wait out here. You can be the getaway driver," Max answered as he climbed out of the Jeep. Michael had seemed basically okay with her when they came out of the bus station, but Max hadn't been able to find out exactly what her deal was yet. Until he did, she wasn't anyone he wanted around in a dangerous situation.

Michael led the group over to the door. "Do I knock or what?"

134

Alex reached out and rang the doorbell. "Candy-gram," he called softly.

Maria started to giggle. She shoved both fists up to her mouth, trying to hold in her laughter.

"Oh, very intimidating," Liz told her.

Her giggling stopped abruptly as the door swung open and a handsome, blue-eyed young man appeared. Max's eyes immediately sought out the man's right hand. He'd been able to regrow the finger.

"I do nice work, don't I?" the young man asked, noticing the direction of Max's gaze. It was DuPris—and his shape-shifting skills were impressive. If he was at all afraid that Max was going to attack him again, he didn't show it.

Max did a quick check of his group, not allowing his eyes to linger on Liz. They were doing pretty well at the show-no-fear thing themselves. "We came to make you an offer," he said.

"Well, do tell," DuPris drawled. As he spoke, his face returned to its usual shape. "I used that ridiculous southern accent for too long. I'm having trouble getting rid of it." He stood away from the door. "If we're going to do business, you might as well come inside."

The place hadn't been used in years. There were sheets over the furniture in the living room DuPris directed them to, and a layer of dust coated the wood floor.

"I'm surprised you were able to find me,"

DuPris admitted. "I didn't think you would have mastered the *lavila* this soon after your *akino*."

Max shrugged. He had no clue what DuPris was talking about, but there was no reason for him to know that. If he wanted to think Max had more powers than he actually did, great.

"You want the ring. We want Adam and Isabel. If they aren't here, we have nothing to talk about," Michael said. The polite chitchat was obviously driving him crazy.

A door at the other end of the living room swung open, and a little boy and girl stepped through. As Max watched, they began to change. The girl's dark hair turned to a deep wine color, then to a rusty brown, then lightened quickly to Isabel's honey blond. Her eyes lightened and brightened to Isabel's blue. Her body stretched up and grew curves, not something Max especially wanted to see. In an instant the transformation was complete.

But not. Isabel's eyes were the right shade of blue, but they were empty. Her face lacked any animation. She and Adam were like the most expensive mannequins ever created.

"Release them," Max ordered. "You're not getting the ring unless you can prove they're unharmed."

"You have a lot of demands," DuPris commented.

"I have the ring," Max answered. A worthless ring that would basically kill anyone who used it.

He hoped his expression wasn't betraying any hint of that little fact.

"You have a point," DuPris conceded.

And then Isabel was running to Max. She grabbed him and held on to him so hard, it hurt. "You're okay," he whispered in her ear. "We'll be out of here in a couple of minutes."

She pulled away. "Is Adam . . . ?"

"I'm here," he answered.

Max turned and saw him standing next to Liz, his green eyes focused and alert. "Good to have you back," Max told him.

"This is all quite touching," DuPris said. "Now give me the ring."

Max reached into his pocket and pulled out the ring. Moment of truth, he thought. He handed it to DuPris.

"Good to have you back," DuPris said to the Stone.

The Stone began to glow, and the hair on Max's arms prickled. It was time to leave—and fast. As Alex had said, they should be standing way, way back at this point. He jerked his chin toward the door.

Michael nodded. "We'll leave you two alone together," he told DuPris.

"That's not necessary. In fact, I won't hear of it," DuPris answered. "I want to try this baby out. I bet with the Stone, I can take control of all of you at the same time. Any takers?"

The living room exploded with the Stone's purple-green light before Max could even consider connecting to the consciousness.

And it was over.

DuPris had him. Had all of them. Max couldn't see the others—his eyes were locked straight ahead—but he knew if even one of them was still free, they'd be attacking DuPris right now.

"That was too easy," DuPris complained as he headed over to Max. "It sort of spoiled the fun." He licked his finger and used it to smooth out Max's eyebrows, then he moved on.

Was he touching Liz now? The thought made Max feel as if he were going insane. He couldn't even turn his head to look at her. Forget his head. He couldn't even move his eyes.

DuPris moved back into his field of vision, his face so close to Max's, it blotted out everything else. "Your girlfriend is delightful," he commented. His tongue flicked out and brushed across his upper lip, as if he was enjoying the taste of something. "But I don't think I'll touch her yet. She's worth savoring."

He can read my thoughts, Max realized.

"Yes, and they're very predictable," DuPris answered. "Very human, I'm afraid to say. Poor Max, all in a knot at the idea that I might get a little too close to Miss Ortecho. Don't worry. Though she *is* very attractive."

Michael could practically feel the fury pouring out of Max, a fury that matched his own.

"Another predictable human response," DuPris said, circling around in front of him. "I must say I'm disappointed in you, although I suppose I must take into account that you were raised here. Well, *raised* is perhaps not the correct word. Pitiful unwanted little Michael, the orphan boy. You haven't had an easy time of it on this planet, have you? Skipping from home to home where no one liked you well enough to keep you." He reached out and straightened Michael's collar. "Don't worry, Mikey boy, I'm going to keep you forever and ever."

Michael wanted to rip off DuPris's head and drop-kick it across the room. Yeah, and then do a victory dance on his body.

DuPris laughed. "Very colorful," he said. "I think you need a demonstration, something to help you adjust to your new circumstances."

Michael's heart began to flutter. Get a grip, he ordered himself. Don't let this clown scare you.

DuPris shook his head. "You're not exactly quick, are you?" he asked.

Michael's heart jerked in his chest. It isn't fear causing this, he realized. It's DuPris. His heart jerked again. A little harder and it could rip the veins and arteries connecting it to his body.

"That's right. And you know what would happen then," DuPris said. "Bu-bye!"

All Michael could do was stand there motionless as his body turned against him. Pain speared up his left arm. His heartbeat doubled, then doubled again, each frantic beat yanking on the veins and arteries.

White dots exploded in front of his eyes. A metallic taste flooded his mouth. Bu-bye! he thought wildly.

And then his heart slowed down. The pain subsided. His vision cleared, and the first thing he saw was the satisfied smile on DuPris's face.

"Consider that the first class of New Reality 101," DuPris told him. "And you will be tested later."

Even if DuPris hadn't had control over her, Maria didn't think she'd have been able to move. The terror would have kept her rooted in place.

"Now that's what I like to hear," DuPris said. "What a good little bunny you are."

She felt a hand pat her on the head. Oh, God, he was right behind her.

"I've always wondered what kinds of thoughts

141

bunnies are capable of having," he continued. "Let me just look around for a minute."

Memories began to flash through Maria's mind. She saw herself lying on her stomach, drawing a lavender pony. Watching her mother get dressed for a date. Buying her first box of tampons. Using a feather duster to wake the other kids in her preschool class up from a nap. Refusing to dissect a worm. Kissing Michael.

"Ah, interesting," DuPris murmured.

The memories continued to race by, but now they were all of Michael. Michael flicking cake batter at her. Michael slow dancing with her. Michael laughing at her imitation of a serial killer on Prozac. Michael staring intently into her eyes. Michael listening to Maria babbling that he had to choose between her and Isabel.

"And even more interesting," DuPris said. "It seems one of my Pinocchios has won the heart of two of my Pinocchiettas. Isn't that sweet?" He patted Maria on the head again.

She felt humiliated. Violated. DuPris had destroyed some of her most precious memories by using them for his entertainment.

"I'll give you a new memory to make up for it," DuPris promised her, continuing to invade her mind.

Maria felt an electric current begin racing through her body, zapping her nerve endings. She made a quarter turn, took two steps, and made another quarter turn. She found herself in front of Michael, her eyes focused on his chest. Without her will, her arms reached toward him.

Maria had spent hours fantasizing about touching Michael again, about him touching her, inventing all kinds of scenarios for how it would happen. Now her daydreams had turned into a nightmare. DuPris was going to make them put their hands on each other while the scumbag got off on the show. Don't make me do this, Maria silently pleaded, hating herself for begging but willing to do anything to stop this.

"Oh, come on," DuPris said. "It's exactly what you want to do, and you know it. And you don't have to worry about Michael rejecting you this time because he can't!"

Maria's arms looped around Michael's neck. His hands wrapped themselves around her waist.

It's just Michael, she thought. He may not have chosen you in the girl-o-rama, but he's still your friend. Whatever happens, remember that it's him touching you, even if DuPris is pulling the strings.

Michael slid one hand lower, tracing the curve of her hip. She wished she could look into his face at least, but DuPris wouldn't even allow that.

It's Michael, she repeated to herself as she was forced to press a mechanical kiss against the side of his jaw. It's Michael.

He pulled her tighter against him, and she caught a whiff of something sharp and tangy.

Eucalyptus. Eucalyptus—what she always smelled when they made a connection.

They weren't completely connected yet, but if they could—Maria slammed the thought away. She couldn't let DuPris read it.

It's Michael. It's Michael. It's Michael. She returned to her mantra, but now it held a new meaning.

"I told you you'd enjoy yourself," DuPris said. She felt him toying with one of her curls, but she refused to let herself be distracted.

Her fingers were forced into Michael's hair, and she tried to imagine her aura wrapping itself around them both. The sent of roses, her connection scent, blended with the eucalyptus, softening its bitter edge.

Almost there, she thought. Then she caught a flicker of blue out of the corner of her eye and a splash of brick red. Their auras were becoming visible to her. They swirled together—and it happened. Michael and Maria made the connection.

She raised her eyes to Michael's. *She* raised her eyes. Not DuPris.

Before DuPris had a chance to realize what had happened, Maria shot her hand to the left and grabbed Isabel by the arm.

An infusion of Maria's sparking blue aura and Michael's brick red one shot into Isabel's body. She could almost taste it in her blood.

She tried to wiggle her fingers and smiled when she was successful. She reached for Max, grabbed his hand, and felt his aura rushing through her, too, giving her a blast of big brother protection along with the smell of cedar. DuPris didn't know who he was dealing with here. When the six of them made a connection, they were unstoppable.

She'd missed Max, missed all of them so much. She felt as if she'd been away from them forever. But she was back!

Hi, Liz, Isabel thought when she felt Liz's amber aura join the rainbow ripping through her. She took a deep breath and caught a touch of Liz's exotic ylang-ylang in the perfume of their connection.

She was totally losing it, but she didn't care. They were going to shatter DuPris's hold on them. And then they'd be free. If she could, she would have done her trademark back flip into a full split. Free! Whee!

"The puppets are trying to take over the theater," DuPris said dryly. "How entertaining."

Give us one more minute, and you'll see how entertaining it is, Isabel thought. She realized DuPris might take it as a challenge if he chose that minute to read her thoughts, but let him. She was ready for a fight.

Alex's vivid orange aura zoomed into the mix, trailing the scent of almonds. The force of it, of *him*, almost knocked Isabel off her feet. Who wouldn't be ready for a fight with Alex on their side? The boy might not have any powers, but he did not know the meaning of the word *surrender.*

Isabel let out a whoop, glorying in her ability to open her mouth and make a sound. She was regaining control by the moment. The room began to fill with music, a concert made up of the music of their dream orbs. She wasn't the only one who was back. They were all back!

Alex threw out an image to the group—a cartoon man in a black-and-white-striped uniform swimming away from Alcatraz, his arms moving as fast as a plane's propellers. Alex knew no one had been held prisoner on the island for years, but hey, why be so literal?

Isabel responded with a picture of herself in her cheerleader uniform, jumping up and down and yelling her head off. Typical Isabel. Had to send a picture of herself. But there was no bitterness to the thought. Here, in the connection, he could open himself up to her without their history weighing him down. He could enjoy the pure, essential Isabel, with all their mutual crap stripped away.

She sent out another picture of herself, this time jumping so high, she touched the sun. Yeah, baby, he thought.

Michael followed up with a surfer shooting a curl. The big cheeseball. Alex shot him back a grinning guy in a T-shirt that said Totally Tubular on the front.

With each image the power of the connection grew stronger. They were charging the battery. Gassing up. Amazing that this little cornball image exchange would turn them into a well-oiled fighting machine.

Adam cringed as Max hurled out the image of a tiger stalking through the jungle, yellow eyes watchful.

This was all too much, too big, too loud. The colors of all the auras clashed with the pictures everyone kept throwing. And the heavy perfume swirling around him felt like it was replacing all the oxygen in the air.

He started to pull his hand away from Liz's, but she held tight. She let an image slowly unfurl in front of him. The two of them in her backyard, just sitting on the grass under the night sky.

Michael sent him a picture of the two of them playing crazy eights in his compound cell. Isabel waited until that image had completely faded, then sent over the acid green clouds of the home planet they shared. Max added a view of the earth from space. Maria showed him a butterfly breaking free of a cocoon, wings still wet.

They wanted him to be a part of this and not just to protect him, he realized. He let his own aura stretch out, adding a band of yellow to the ribbons of color tying them together.

He took a deep breath, allowing himself to appreciate each scent in the air, including the smell of green leaves that he somehow knew was coming from him. Then he selected an image and let it soar out. He smiled as the two pieces of golden brown toast popped out of the shiny silver toaster.

His smile widened as Alex responded with the image of all seven of them eating toast together. Loaves and loaves of perfect toast.

Liz could actually taste the buttery toast in her mouth. This felt so right, all of it.

"Are you about finished?" DuPris asked. The image of the whole group eating toast shriveled as he paced in front of them. "It seems that it's already time for another lesson in New Reality 101."

She tightened her grip on Max and Adam. They were still connected, and the connection was still strong. But not strong enough to take on DuPris. Not yet. She could feel it.

Liz chose another image—Max healing her after she got shot at the Crashdown. That's where it all started. That's what brought them all together, even Adam, in a way, because that day they all started down the road that led to him.

She catapulted out the image, but she couldn't feel a response. It didn't reach them, not even Max, she realized.

"I hold in my hand one of the three Stones of

Midnight," DuPris lectured. "Its power is greater than anything you have ever experienced. Until now."

Liz felt her stomach lurch, and she realized the house, the entire house, was rising into the air. A moment later it fell with a shuddering crash that sent Liz's teeth slamming together. She swallowed and tasted blood in her mouth.

"That was just a little demonstration. Very little," he continued. "Ready for another one?"

Yeah, Liz thought. Bring it to us. That will bring the—

She stopped herself from completing the thought in case DuPris was listening.

"I can feel the peanut of power you've got growing over there. Want to see what it can do?" he asked. "I think we should all see what it can do." He yanked Maria out of the group.

Isabel and Michael immediately closed the gap, but Liz felt cold without the warmth of Maria's aura around her. The music of the connection sounded out of key without her note. The perfume smelled too sharp and spicy.

There's still a lot of strength left, she told herself. But she felt so powerless seeing Maria standing next to DuPris, her eyes blank and dead.

"Don't worry, I'm not going to hurt her," he announced. "She's just going to be the prize in a game I call bunny, bunny, who's got the bunny. Here's how it works. You use your power to keep me from taking back full control. I use my power to make you the puppet people. You win, you can leave. You lose, and the bunny gets burned." He patted Maria on the head. "And you'll do the burning."

No, Liz thought. Not that. If she did anything to hurt Maria, she wouldn't want to live herself.

DuPris turned to Adam. "You remember the rules, don't you? You and I played once before. Or was it twice?"

Liz felt a shudder course through Adam, and the connection grew a little shakier. We're weakening, and we haven't even really started yet, she thought.

DuPris beamed and opened his arms wide. "Okay, ready, one, two, three—go!"

She braced herself for a blast of the Stone's power. It didn't come.

Don't think about it, she ordered herself. Build up the connection. That's the only thing that matters.

But how? She turned her attention to the bands of color binding them together. She didn't know what to do exactly, but she had to try something. She imagined their auras turning to metal, using all her will to make them hard and strong, impenetrable.

And it began to work. She didn't know how. She suspected that the connection helped her to access a power that she'd always had, maybe locked in one of those mysterious pieces of the human brain that seemed to have no function.

Liz felt the others join with her, struggling to

turn the rays of light into armor. When the armor was finished, DuPris would have no control over them. She hoped.

She discovered it was most effective to concentrate on reinforcing her own aura. She focused her mind on the bands of amber, working her way inch by inch, not allowing anything to distract her.

Until she noticed the beads of moisture on the piece of aura she had just finished. The droplets gleamed with the Stone's purple-green light.

And they ate through the armor like acid.

Cameron stared at the ranch house. It had flown probably twenty feet in the air before it crashed. And it was a *house*. What the hell were they fighting in there?

Cameron sidled up to the closest window and peeked inside. The scene inside was utterly confusing. Michael and the others were surrounded by what looked like big sheets of metal that were being eaten away by acid or something. Cameron wasn't sure if that was good or bad.

Maria stood apart from them, and it was clear she'd entered the zombie zone. Clearly bad.

And there was a guy with oily, slicked-back hair holding a glowing stone. Obviously he's the one I should go after, she decided. She circled around to the back of the house, found an unlocked door, and slipped inside.

You have no weapon of any kind. You have no martial arts training. You don't even have very long fingernails. Just what are you planning to do? she asked herself as she made her way through the kitchen and down a dark hall. She had no answer.

"Honey, I'm home," she muttered under her breath as she stepped up to the half-open door that she thought was the one she'd seen from outside. If she went in here, she should end up behind the oily-haired guy with about half the room between them.

At least until he turned around and threw her farther than he'd thrown the house.

Cameron knew if she stood there much longer, she'd wuss out. She shoved open the door and ran toward the man as fast as she could. She pretended the couch was a track hurdle and leaped over it.

Her outstretched leg slammed into the back of the guy's head and knocked him to the ground. Cameron landed beside him. Which was pretty much the end of her nonexistent plan.

The eroded metal surrounding the group clattered to the floor, and Michael stumbled forward. It took a second for him to realize that he had total control of his body again.

Immediately he whipped his head toward Maria. She was free, too, already holding on to Liz with both hands.

And DuPris? Michael spotted him lying on the floor next to . . . Cameron. What? When did she— Didn't matter. She was here, and somehow she'd managed to bring down DuPris.

But not for long. DuPris was already struggling to his feet, his eyes locked on her.

"Cameron, get over here!" Michael shouted. And then he felt his stomach clench into a ball. Her right leg was twisted at an impossible angle. It had to be broken.

"Cover me!" Michael shouted. Without waiting for an answer, he hurled himself at Cameron. He wrapped his arms around her and rolled them both across the floor. A bolt of sizzling green-purple lightning struck about a foot away from them.

"I said, cover me!" he yelled.

Max didn't want to kill DuPris, but if it was DuPris or Michael—"Listen up, everyone!" he called. "DuPris is the bunny."

Instantly he felt a ball of power begin to form in the middle of the group. There wasn't time to let it get too big. Michael and Cameron couldn't wait for their backup. DuPris looked ready to hurl another lightning bolt. Max could see it forming.

"Okay, now!" he shouted. The air crackled as they hurled the ball at DuPris's head.

DuPris spun toward it and raised the ring. The ball exploded in a harmless shower of sparks—and

DuPris turned back to Michael and Cameron, the new bolt of lightning fully formed in his hand.

"Michael, move!" Max shouted.

Michael pulled Cameron over in another roll—and they hit the wall.

DuPris drew back his arm.

A wave of coldness washed over Max. There was no time for another attack. He wasn't going to be able to save them.

A blast shook the room, brilliant white light filling every corner, dazzling Max's eyes. "Michael, are you guys all right?" he shouted. "Did you get hit?" He blinked rapidly, trying to clear his vision.

Two beings came into view, moving slowly across the living room toward DuPris. They were tall and thin, their legs and arms extremely long.

And their mouths . . . Max couldn't stop staring at their mouths. They were gaping holes lined with pencil-thick tentacles, tentacles that continuously waved from side to side as if tasting the air.

"The bounty hunters," Maria breathed.

Game over, DuPris, Max thought. And guess what? You lose! Because the bounty hunters—our saviors—are about to take you back home for judgment. And finally, thank God, we will be safe.

DuPris glanced over his shoulder and smiled with relief. "It took you two long enough," he complained. "I've been waiting for over fifty years."

10

DuPris knows the bounty hunters. They're not here to kill him. They're here to *help* him. The realization was like a fist to Max's kidneys. Another realization quickly followed—he was going to have to open the wormhole.

But not now. It was too dangerous without the element of surprise on his side. Right now, DuPris was all caught up in reaming out the hunters, but any second he could turn his attention back to the group. They could hardly hold off DuPris while he used the ring. There was no way they'd be able to fight him *and* these vicious-looking bounty hunters.

Max decided to use the momentary distraction of the hunters to reconnect the group.

"Everybody grab hands . . . now," Max ordered.

The group quickly re-formed the circle—including Michael, who had Cameron cradled in his arms. She was connected now, too. An olive green aura had joined the colors wrapped around them.

Max sent out an image—a stream of molecules rushing from the ranch house all the way back to the UFO museum.

"Max, no!" Liz cried.

But he didn't have time to come up with something better. He'd have to do it on his own, too, without the consciousness. He'd need all their strength later . . . and it still might not be enough to survive opening the wormhole.

He shoved the thought away. Right now, all you have to do is move some molecules, he told himself. Nothing you haven't done before. Except this time he'd be trying to re-form himself. Michael wouldn't be there to do it for him.

Max focused on his body, on *their* body. He could feel all eight of their hearts beating. He visualized the museum, picking the exact spot he wanted them to go, then he gave their molecules a mighty *shove,* scattering them like pool balls after the break.

He felt himself flying apart, his molecules mixing with the molecules of Liz, Michael, Alex, Isabel, Maria, Adam, and Cameron. No, more than that— mixing with the molecules that made up the world. Everything was molecules, and he was everything.

His consciousness, his *Maxness,* felt as if it was disappearing. For a moment he fought it, resisting the pull toward oneness, then he abandoned himself to it, throwing himself into the void. So this is freedom was the last thought he was able to form.

"That was so cool!" Maria cried.

Max opened his eyes, feeling shaky with relief.

He'd done it. He didn't know how, but he'd done it. All eight of them were standing in the museum's little coffee shop.

Liz shook her head. "It should have been impossible. How could you have re-formed us when your own brain was in pieces?"

"You even put my leg back the right way," Cameron added. She kicked her leg out a few times. "No broken bone."

"And you managed to bring our clothes," Michael said. "What a guy."

"I didn't bring the Jeep, though," Max answered. "I guess I'll have to tell Dad that Isabel left the keys in it again and someone stole it." He glanced over at his sister. She had her eyes lowered, and he could tell she hadn't even heard what he'd said. She just needs a little decompression time, he thought.

"I have a theory—well, not about the clothes part, but about the other part. Want to hear my theory?" Maria asked. She bounced back and forth on her toes, obviously enjoying an adrenaline high.

Max smiled at her. "I would love to hear your theory." In fact, there was nothing he'd like more. He wanted to stand here for a minute and hang with his friends like a normal person.

"There are some massage therapists who believe memory is stored in the body, not just in the brain," Maria explained. "Supposedly they can help people tap into a repressed memory just by touching them in the right place. Anyway, I think maybe our molecules remembered where they belonged."

"Either that or the molecule fairy put them back together for us," Alex said.

"Molecule fairy?" Adam repeated, a faint frown on his face.

Max was struck by just how few days Adam had had in the real world. He had a lot of lost time to make up for. Max promised himself he'd help him do it.

"Adam, there's something you have to know about Alex," Michael told him. "He's a moron."

Everyone laughed except Isabel. "So what do we do now?" she asked, her voice harsh.

Max rubbed the back of his neck. "The wormhole," he answered. "I don't think we have any choice." He braced himself for another round of protests. They didn't come. Probably because they'd all gotten a firsthand look at how phenomenally powerful DuPris was, how impossible it would be for them to come up with a plan to defeat him.

"When?" Liz asked, wrapping her arms around her waist.

"As soon as we can figure out a way to catch DuPris a little off guard," Max answered. "Any ideas?"

"We could all dress up like hookers," Alex suggested, voice flat.

"I think we should eat, get some rest, then meet up and start working on a plan," Liz said.

"We don't have time for that," Michael answered, his voice grim. "Look!"

Max followed Michael's gaze and saw a network of veins forming a few feet away. "DuPris followed us!" he cried.

"Not just DuPris," Michael shot back. And Max realized there were two other bodies beginning to form—the hunters.

"How long will it take you to open the wormhole?" Alex demanded.

"I don't know," Max admitted.

"Go upstairs and start the process," Liz ordered. "Ray's bedroom is pretty much over the coffee shop. We'll keep DuPris in here. You open the hole above him."

"How are you going—," Max began to protest.

"Let us worry about that!" Liz exclaimed. "Now go!"

Max ran for the staircase. Liz checked on DuPris. His organs had formed, but he still had no eyes. "Michael, Isabel, Adam, make all of us look like DuPris!" she cried.

"What good will that do?" Isabel yelled.

"I don't know. But we have to try something, and maybe we can confuse the hunters," Liz explained in a rush. "They won't attack us if they think there's a possibility we're DuPris."

Adam stepped up in front of her and put his hands on her face. She felt her flesh begin to shift, her bones softening and re-forming in a new configuration. Out of the corner of her eye she saw Michael working on Cameron. She glanced in the other direction. Isabel already had Alex and Maria looking exactly like DuPris.

"Done," Adam announced.

"Do yourself. Hurry!" Liz urged. Flesh was covering DuPris's body and the long, thin frames of the bounty hunters. But DuPris's eye sockets were still empty, and the dozens of little bumps that were the bounty hunters' eyes hadn't formed yet.

"Now what?" Isabel asked.

"Now we try to buy Max some time," Liz answered. She forced herself to stand right next to DuPris, and she was the first thing he looked at when his eyes formed.

"I'm tired of games," he told her. He reached for her throat.

"Are you two lumps going to stand there while he attacks me?" she yelled at the bounty hunters, striving for DuPris's arrogant tone. "Kill him!"

The bounty hunters responded immediately, so fast on their long legs. One of them grabbed DuPris by the hair.

"Touch me again and I'll turn you into ash right now," DuPris barked. The bounty hunter let go. DuPris pointed at Liz. "That one is an imposter. Destroy it!"

"Both of them are impostors!" another voice that sounded like DuPris's called from behind her. "Leave them and follow me!"

The hunters hesitated, looking at each other. Then one moved up to DuPris and one moved up to Liz. It leaned close, closer.

Hurry up, Max, she thought. She squeezed her eyes shut as the hunter began using its mouth tentacles to explore her face.

Max felt the consciousness pulling the power out of him, stretching it out and up as they frantically tried to construct a tunnel between his world and theirs.

He knew only part of the power for the wormhole had to come from him. The power of the consciousness would create one piece of the tunnel.

But he was exhausted, and he wasn't sure he had enough power in him to make this work. He tried not to resist as the consciousness yanked more power from him. He thought he could feel his body withering on the inside, as if blood and other vital fluids were somehow being taken out of him, too.

You're imagining it, he told himself. But he hadn't imagined the dried-out spot on his neck. The process, whatever it was, obviously had an effect on his body.

There's no other way to get DuPris back, he reminded himself, gritting his teeth as the power was drawn out of him even more rapidly.

He heard a sucking sound, and for a second he thought he was actually hearing his power being siphoned from his body. Then he realized that it was the sound of the wormhole beginning to open.

Max tried to swallow, but there was no saliva left in his mouth. His tongue felt like a hunk of sandpaper.

There wasn't much left in him, he realized. Not much power. Not much of anything.

He just had to hope there was enough to finish opening the hole.

Isabel shot a glance at the swirling spot in the ceiling almost directly over Liz's and DuPris's heads. It was as if the plaster in the spot had turned to thick pudding that was being stirred by an invisible spoon. It had to be the wormhole beginning to open. Anytime now, Max, she thought.

She returned her gaze to Liz and the bounty hunter. It was using one of its tentacles to trace the inside of her ear. Even watching sent shivers of revulsion through Isabel.

"I told you, I'm over here!" Isabel shouted. "Come on! We have work to do!"

The hunters didn't respond. They'd clearly decided to examine the first two DuPrises completely before they did anything else. Would Liz's disguise fool them? Why hasn't DuPris shifted shape again? She assumed, from the worn expression on his face, that he had exhausted too much of his power to shape-shift again. Or maybe DuPris knew there was something in Liz's scent or shape that would give her away.

Isabel hated just standing there watching. She wondered if she should slip away and go upstairs. Maybe Max needed help opening the wormhole.

Or maybe the attempt had already drained him to the point of death.

That settled it. She was going. She turned, then she heard a sound that turned her bones to ice—a wheezing, hiccuping, unnatural sound.

Isabel spun back to face Liz and realized that the sound was coming from the bounty hunter in front of her friend. It's . . . it's laughing, she realized.

"I told you it was the imposter," DuPris snapped. "Now are you going to kill it, or do I have to do everything myself?"

"Look!" Alex shouted—at least Isabel was pretty sure it was Alex. They all sounded exactly alike with the changes in their vocal cords. He pointed to the ceiling.

Isabel tilted back her head. The swirling spot was almost transparent now.

The bounty hunters made gibbering sounds of fear and darted to the far wall. Liz bolted over to Isabel's side. DuPris stared up, motionless, transfixed. Then he began to back away, his eyes never leaving the ceiling. He knocked into Isabel, but he didn't seem to notice.

With a deep sucking sound, the spot in the ceiling opened completely. Isabel's ears popped as the pressure in the room changed.

"No! I'm not going back," DuPris screamed from behind her. But he seemed unable to run.

One of the little tables slid across the floor, metal legs squealing. It spun around under the hole, then flew straight up and disappeared. Liz grabbed Isabel by the wrist and pulled her down. "Lie flat on your stomach," she cried. "It will be harder for it to suck you in."

"What about DuPris? We have to get him in there," Isabel shouted. Another table was sucked up through the hole in the ceiling.

Michael crawled over—at least Isabel thought it was Michael. "Connect with me," he called, looping his arm across her and Liz. "Maybe we can use our power to push him through from here."

Isabel glanced over his shoulder, her oily DuPris hair whipping around her face. "DuPris is still just standing there. What is he doing?"

DuPris gave a howl of anguish. "Help me!" he wailed. But he started sliding toward the spot below the hole, like some kind of barefoot water-skier.

Isabel realized they weren't going to have to do anything but watch. The force of the wormhole had him.

"Help me!" DuPris cried. "Help me!" His arms pinwheeled as he struggled to fight the suction. "I don't want to go. . . ."

But it was too late. His feet were lifted off the ground as the suction of the hole pulled him up.

The bounty hunters let out shrill screams. They

darted over and grabbed DuPris by the legs. DuPris shrieked as if his body were being ripped in two, but the hunters didn't let go.

An instant later all three of them disappeared into the wormhole.

"We have to get out of here," Michael cried. "Stay low."

Isabel struggled to turn around while keeping her body pressed tight against the floor, then she began to crawl, fighting against the pull of the hole. She felt one of her shoes fly off and tried not to think about her whole body flying after it.

"This helps," she heard Liz yell.

She turned her head, her eyes stinging from all the dust and debris whizzing past her. Liz was using the metal stools lining the counter to pull herself along.

Great idea. They were bolted to the floor. Isabel rolled over and grabbed the closest one. Pulling herself hand over hand, she made it to the end of the coffee shop. Then she pushed herself into a crouch and ran as fast as she could while keeping her body low.

Liz and Michael were already halfway to the staircase. Isabel checked over her shoulder. Four DuPrises were right behind her. Good, no one got sucked!

She raced over to the stairs and took them three at a time. She had to be sure Max was all right.

"Everybody link up before we go in," Michael ordered from in front of the bedroom door. "We might

165

need each other to fight the pull of the hole, or . . ."

He didn't finish the sentence. He didn't have to. Isabel knew exactly what he was thinking—they might need the power of the connection to try to save Max's life.

She reached out and grabbed the two closest hands. The connection began to form immediately. But it felt different somehow. Almost tainted.

We're all totally freaked. Of course it infects the connection a little, she thought.

She shook off the thought as Michael pushed open the bedroom door and led the way inside. Isabel felt tears begin to stream down her face the moment she saw her brother. He was almost unrecognizable. The skin of his face had hardened into deep furrows, and his body wasn't much more than bones covered by dry, dry skin.

"You've got to help me close the hole," he choked out.

She rushed over to him and pressed her hands against his neck. The others joined her, placing their hands on Max, too, centering their connection in his body.

"I think if we can break Max free of the consciousness, the hole will close," Isabel shouted, her voice almost overpowered by the sucking of the wormhole.

She gathered up her energy and blasted out an image of Max teaching her how to ride a bike. You're Max, she thought. Max. My big brother. You're not some little insignificant piece of the consciousness.

She chose another memory—Max dressed up as a mad scientist for Halloween—and shot it out. You're Max, the science geek.

The others started showing Max images of himself, too. Images of Max the boyfriend. Max the best friend. Max the son. Max the mouse healer. Max the teacher of the toaster. Max the saint. Max the heart of their group.

The horrible sucking sound of the wormhole lessened. "It's working," Liz cried. "Keep going."

Liz was right. The patch of skin under Isabel's fingers was growing softer and fleshier, as if it was rehydrating. "We need you more than the consciousness does, Max," she yelled. That should get him. Mr. Responsibility.

She grinned as the wormhole snapped shut. The grin practically stretched to her ears when Max sat up. "You look almost like a person again," she told him. He still had a few of those freakish withered spots, but he really did look basically okay.

"He looks a lot better than I do," one of the DuPrises complained.

Max's eyes widened as he took in their appearance. "I can fix that," he said. He reached out and touched the whiny DuPris's face. A few moments later Maria had her own look back. She gave her blond curls a happy shake.

Isabel reached up and pressed her fingers

167

against her forehead, disgusted by the feel of the oily hair. She started to change herself back. "The guy should rethink his styling products," she complained, the words coming out distorted as the DuPris lips changed into her own.

"I don't think he'll have to worry about it where he is," Max answered. "He probably doesn't even have hair anymore."

Isabel glanced around. Only one DuPris left to go—Alex. She felt a pang of self-consciousness about touching him. It felt sort of weird again now that they weren't fighting for their lives. She told herself to get over it and reached out and cupped Alex's face in her hands.

Alex snickered. "Am I tickling you?" she asked.

He didn't answer. He just narrowed his eyes and glared at her as she began concentrating on moving the molecules back in the right place.

Isabel stared at him. She couldn't get his face to change back.

"Having trouble? That's because there's no point in changing me . . . into me!" he shouted, his eyes bulging. "I hope your friend likes his new planet!" DuPris said as he dashed out of the room.

Isabel started to tremble. "What have we done?" she asked.

Max replied slowly, "We sent Alex through the wormhole."

SIX TEENS,
ONE SECRET . . .

Max loves **Liz**, but he can't let her get too close . . .

Alex wants **Isabel**—but is she just using him?

Maria always daydreams about **Michael**. But will he ever stop thinking of her as a little sister?

Don't miss the next Roswell High:

THE VANISHED

Max is on a mission. He has to save Alex, who is stranded on the home planet. To bring his human friend back, Max knows he'll need the Stone of Midnight. If only he knew where to look. . . .

Liz misses her boyfriend. Max has been so consumed with finding Alex that he never spends time with her anymore. And she understands. Especially because she's been busy, too—helping Adam adjust to life in Roswell. It's just that . . . she's enjoying her time with Adam a little *too* much.

Look for Roswell High #8,
THE REBEL
Coming soon!

Bullying.
Threats.
Bullets.

Locker searches? Metal detectors?

Fight back without fists.